"Are you still interested in the position?"

She gave him a surprised look. "Are you interested in me *taking* the position?"

The incredulity in her voice made him feel like a piece of gum on the bottom of her shoe. He hadn't disappeared on her back then because he didn't like her—quite the opposite, really. But he absolutely didn't have the energy to go into any of that right now.

"Aunt Mabel said there's only been one person who's replied to the job posting so far." He paused. "You."

She crossed her arms over her chest. "I'm moving to Boston after Christmas, so this wouldn't be long-term."

Steve hadn't been aware that his shoulders were tight, but he felt them loosen in relief. "Temporary is fine. He'll be old enough for day care in the New Year. I just really need to get back to work."

Chloe nodded. "All right. When do you want me to start?"

He shifted the baby so he could take a quick glance at his watch. "How about now?"

Meghann Whistler grew up in Canada but spent her summers on the beaches of Cape Cod. Before settling down with her rocket scientist husband and raising three rambunctious boys, she worked variously as a magazine writer, a model and a marketing communications manager at a software company. She loves to hear from her readers, who can reach her at www.meghannwhistler.com.

Books by Meghann Whistler

Love Inspired

Falling for the Innkeeper
The Baby's Christmas Blessing

Visit the Author Profile page at LoveInspired.com.

The Baby's Christmas Blessing

Meghann Whistler

LOVE INSPIRED
INSPIRATIONAL ROMANCE

LOVE INSPIRED®
INSPIRATIONAL ROMANCE

Recycling programs
for this product may
not exist in your area.

ISBN-13: 978-1-335-58606-3

The Baby's Christmas Blessing

Copyright © 2022 by Meghann Whistler

For questions and comments about the quality of this book, please contact us at CustomerService@Harlequin.com.

Love Inspired
22 Adelaide St. West, 41st Floor
Toronto, Ontario M5H 4E3, Canada
www.LoveInspired.com

Printed in U.S.A.

Stand fast therefore in the liberty
wherewith Christ hath made us free, and
be not entangled again with the yoke of bondage.
—*Galatians* 5:1

For my sister, who has always dreamed
of creating Christmas-in-a-Can :)

Acknowledgments

Thank you, dear readers, for your support
over the past two years. Reading your sweet
notes and emails, interacting with you on
Facebook and seeing your book reviews has
been a true joy! Thank you for welcoming me
to the Love Inspired family with open arms.

Thank you, as well, to Melissa Endlich and the
Love Inspired team for believing in my work
and bringing it to readers around the world.
I appreciate everything you do!

I'm grateful to my amazing critique partner,
Beth Pugh, for giving this manuscript
an early look. My thanks also go to my
friend Nicholas Holahan and my brother, Mike,
for their help with book-related research.
Most of all, thank you to my husband, Paul,
who never thought he'd read a romance novel
but has now read all of mine!

Finally, thank you to God for giving me the
opportunity to tell stories that bring hope and
happiness to others. I pray that everyone who
reads this book will feel a tiny bit closer to You.

Chapter One

Chloe Richardson gazed down at the baby in her arms. She wanted this job. She *really* wanted this job.

For one thing, the baby was adorable, with his downy hair, silken skin, sweet little lips and teeny-tiny eyelashes. He smelled good, too. Sweet and clean. Like fabric softener for the soul.

Plus, she needed the money. Her student teaching placement was starting in just a few weeks—in Boston, where the cost of living was sky-high—and the restaurant she and her brother, Brett, had inherited from their parents had just closed for renovations.

Which meant Chloe had no money coming in, and no way to save up for an apartment in Boston.

"He likes you," Mabel pronounced, smiling,

her voice quavery, her cane leaning against the side of her armchair.

Chloe looked up. The older woman had short hair that hadn't gone completely gray, glasses that hung around her neck on a chain, and swollen, arthritic knuckles. She was wearing a pink cardigan set over a pair of black slacks, with a bejeweled cat brooch attached to her lapel.

Chloe herself—who was dressed much more casually in jeans and a red Christmas sweater with faux fur trim—would have worn that brooch. Although she didn't wear it much anymore, she'd always liked costume jewelry.

Smoothing her finger over the baby's soft cheek, she told Mabel, "I like him, too."

"Does that mean you'll take the job?" Mabel leaned forward in her seat, an expectant look on her face.

Chloe sighed. "You know I'm only here for another few weeks, right, Mabel? I'm leaving right after Christmas. You'll hire me just to turn around and have to hire someone else."

Although she definitely wanted the job, she didn't want the baby to suffer because he got attached to her when she wasn't going to be around long. Poor little guy was only two weeks old and he'd already lost his mother to a stroke during childbirth. Chloe had honestly never realized that strokes happened to young people. She'd always thought they only struck the elderly.

For the baby's sake, she wished she'd been right about that.

"Yes, dear. Irene told me about those online classes you've been taking. I just don't understand why you have to go to Boston to finish your teaching degree."

After backing out of her student teaching placement at the last minute this past semester at the request of her then boyfriend, Dan, Chloe had felt fortunate to get any placement for January at all. She'd never aspired to city living, but she'd been struggling with depression since the breakup, and she was hopeful that a change of scenery would help. "It's just— I've always wanted to be a teacher, and I've put it off for so long. I'm finally in a place where I can chase that dream. It's now or never, Mabel. I *have* to go."

"Fair enough, sweetheart. Fair enough."

Mabel leaned forward to lift her glass of water from the coffee table. Her hand shook as she brought it to her mouth. When she tried to place it back down on the coaster, the glass tipped, spilling its contents on the floor. "Oh, no," she said, her brow creasing.

Chloe stood smoothly so as not to jostle the

baby. "Don't worry. I'll put Aiden in his bassinet and then clean it up for you."

Mabel smiled gratefully as Chloe proceeded to mop up the spill. "Do you see why we need you, dear? Even if it's just for a few weeks while we search for someone who can take the job on a permanent basis, we need help now."

"And the baby's father...?"

Mabel shook her head. "Not his father. His uncle."

"Oh," Chloe said. "Where's his father?"

Mabel gave her a rueful glance. "We don't know, sweetheart. Eloise never told any of us his name. I'm not sure she even knew who the father was."

Chloe winged up a quick prayer. Not only had the kid lost his mother, but he was fatherless, too. *God, help this baby. Protect this baby. Let him know love.*

Mabel kept talking. "But Steven's a good man. He'll be a good father to Aiden."

"And he and the baby will live with you here?" Chloe asked skeptically, glancing around the cozy interior of Mabel's beachfront cottage. It was hard to imagine that a grown man would be comfortable staying here for any length of time.

For one thing, it was small. The four-foot-tall, silver-tinsel Christmas tree in the corner swallowed up about half the open space in the little living room. For another, it was…frilly. Mabel had lace curtains, hand-crocheted table toppers and a souvenir spoon collection mounted on the wall.

"Oh, no, no. He has his own place out on Frog Pond. He had a meeting with the bank today. He just dropped Aiden off for an hour so he could take care of that."

"Frog Pond?" Chloe repeated, an icy feeling coming over her.

Once upon a time, she'd known a guy named Steve who'd spent the summer at a cottage on Frog Pond.

Once upon a time, she'd thought she was in love with a guy named Steve who'd spent the summer at a cottage on Frog Pond.

How young and naïve she'd been, letting him kiss her at that farewell bonfire under the stars. Her first kiss. Her most memorable kiss.

And then he'd never called.

"What's the matter, dear?" Mabel asked. "You seem worried all of a sudden."

"Won't your…um, Steven want to interview the nanny candidates himself?"

Mabel chuckled. "That boy has no idea what to look for in a nanny. Besides, he's completely overwhelmed right now, between caring for Aiden all night long and trying to get his new physical therapy practice up and running. Believe me, he doesn't care who I hire. He just wants help."

"All right," Chloe said slowly. "If you're okay with this being a temporary arrangement, you know I need the work now that the restaurant's closed."

Mabel put a shaky, dramatic hand to her heart, and Chloe wondered how desperate this Steven guy had to be to leave the baby with Mabel, whose arthritis was so bad she could barely walk, let alone hold a baby. "Oh, I'm so relieved."

Aiden started crying and Chloe retrieved him from his bassinet. "Don't cry, little guy," she said, rocking him, her voice going high, the way it always did when she spoke to young children. "What's the matter? Are you hungry?"

"His formula's in the kitchen," Mabel said. "Everything you'll need is in his diaper bag."

Chloe nodded, holding Aiden in one arm and snatching up his bouncy chair with the other so she'd have a place to put him while she made his bottle. She wondered how much he weighed. He felt so tiny.

She set the bouncy chair down on the floor in Mabel's little kitchen. Aiden cried harder when she clipped him into the seat. "I'm sorry, baby. It's just for a second, okay?"

She quickly located the diaper bag and extracted a can of powdered formula, a clean bottle and a two-ounce vial of nursery water. "Hmm," she said to herself over the crying, "you need more than two ounces, don't you?" She rooted around in the diaper bag and found a second vial. "Let's try four and see what happens."

She poured the water into the bottle and added two scoops of formula. Then she screwed a cap on the bottle and proceeded to shake the mixture up.

Aiden was really crying now, his face red and tear-streaked. "Just one more second, sweetie," she cooed as she put the fancy venting tube into the bottle and then affixed the nipple to the top. "Hold on one…more…second."

Setting the bottle on the counter, she plucked Aiden from his chair and settled him in her arms, which was a challenge, since he was squirming while he screamed. Once she had a firm hold of him, she grabbed the bottle and tipped it into his mouth.

But she must not have fastened the top of the bottle properly, because the formula didn't trickle gently into his mouth—it dumped out all over his face.

He screamed louder, absolutely irate.

"Oh, no, no, no," Chloe gasped, desperately searching for the paper towels. "I'm sorry. I'm so sorry."

"Um, excuse me," a deep male voice sounded from the entrance to the kitchen, "but what exactly are you doing to my baby?"

When the harried, pint-sized blonde with overgrown bangs and dark, expressive eyes looked up at him, Steve Weston almost took a step backward.

Chloe Richardson.

She looked much more put-together than she had when they were teenagers—back then her fashion sense had been…eclectic, for lack of a better word—but he'd recognize her anywhere.

It had been eleven years since he'd last seen her and yet he'd thought of her often. Her cheerfulness, her helpfulness, her smile.

What was Chloe Richardson doing in his great-aunt's kitchen, holding his newborn nephew? And why was there formula all over his nephew's scrunched-up little face?

"I'm sorry," she said, obviously flustered. "I must not have screwed the bottle top on correctly."

Steve sighed—was she the nanny candidate his great-aunt had found? Could this day get any more complicated? Then he held out his hands. "Give him to me."

She handed Aiden over. Steve used his shirt-sleeve to wipe the baby's face and then put him on his shoulder, careful to support his little head. "Calm down, buddy," he said, doing the bounce-walk that he'd already discovered to be extremely helpful in quieting Aiden when he was upset. "She'll make you another one."

He flicked a glance at Chloe to confirm that she would, indeed, fix a new bottle for the baby. She gave him a quick nod and set to work.

Steve kept bouncing and murmuring reassurances to Aiden, who was still giving those gut-wrenching *don't you dare ignore me* cries. At least when he was forced to pay attention to his nephew, Steve didn't have time to worry about his disastrous meeting at the bank.

When Chloe finally handed over the new bottle, Steve sat and attempted to give it to Aiden, but the baby was too worked up to even try to feed.

Steve gave her a helpless look. "He's really mad."

She blanched. "I'm so sorry."

He winced. It hadn't been his intention to make her feel bad. "I'm not blaming you. I'm just not sure what to do. I'm really new at this whole baby thing."

"We could try taking him outside. Sometimes a change of scenery helps."

Steve got up, Aiden still squalling in his arms. "Okay."

Chloe pushed open the door from the kitchen to his great-aunt's small backyard. Since her house was so close to the beach, the grass was sparse and the soil was sandy. There had been frost on the ground last week, but the weather had warmed since then. It had to be almost sixty degrees out, even though it was early December.

"Come on, buddy," Steve said, walking and bouncing, walking and bouncing. "Everything's okay. The new bottle's ready. You're gonna be fine."

It took a few minutes, but after a while, Aiden's crying took on a less hysterical edge.

Chloe held out the bottle and motioned toward the patio set. "Want to try again?"

Steve took the bottle and sat. This time, Aiden latched right on.

"Phew," Steve said. "The sweet sound of silence."

"I really am sorry about that…"

Steve gave his head a quick shake. "Not your fault. I think those bottles were designed by a rocket scientist."

Her lips quirked into a small smile. He was glad she was feeling better, although he still wasn't entirely sure why she'd been in the kitchen trying to feed Aiden in the first place.

"So, um…what are you doing here, Chloe?" He knew that Aunt Mabel had scheduled an interview with the lone candidate who'd applied for the nanny position, but seriously? That lone candidate was Chloe Richardson?

Chloe's big brown eyes went wide. "You remember me?"

"Of course I remember you, Blondie," he said, using the nickname all the kids at church camp had called her back in the day.

"Oh." A flicker of hurt and confusion flashed across her face. "I thought…"

She seemed to think he'd forgotten all about her, and Steve knew why. His seventeen-year-old self had been a real coward. He never should have kissed her in the first place, and after he had, he should have had enough courage to call her and tell her why things could never work out between them instead of disappearing without a trace.

But what was done was done. There was no changing it now.

Aiden finished feeding, and Steve stood and patted him on the back. "So, did Aunt Mabel ask you to come over to talk about the nanny job?"

Chloe looked away. "We were talking about it, yes…"

"But you didn't know you'd be working for me, did you?"

She looked up at him and shook her head, her

dirty-blond bangs falling into her dark eyes and making Steve's breath catch in his throat. *Still so beautiful.* "I didn't even know you were back on Cape Cod."

Steve scraped a hand over the spiky hairs on the back of his neck. The beautiful girl he'd known had turned into a beautiful woman, but he couldn't afford to be pulled back into her orbit right now.

He desperately needed to find a nanny for Aiden so he could get back to work in his new physical therapy clinic—the very expensive new clinic he'd purchased with the help of a gigantic bank loan—but his great-aunt obviously hadn't known that the two of them had a history.

"Are you…um, still interested in the position?"

She gave him a surprised look. "Are you interested in me *taking* the position?"

The incredulity in her voice made him feel like a piece of gum on the bottom of her shoe. He hadn't disappeared on her back then because he didn't like her—quite the opposite, really. But he absolutely didn't have the energy to go into any of that right now.

"I know it's probably not the ideal situation, but I'm in a real bind. My sister was going to watch the baby while I went to work, but now she's gone and…" He swallowed hard against the lump in his throat.

Ever since the OB/GYN had come out of Eloise's hospital room to deliver the bad news, it felt like he'd been treading water. When Aunt Mabel had told him she'd find a nanny for the baby, it had been a huge relief. But now…

He shook his head. What a horrendous couple of weeks. The worst since his father had… done what he'd done. It almost made Steve wish he'd never come back to Wychmere Bay in the first place.

But he and Eloise had agreed that this would be the best place to raise Aiden, and Steve wasn't going to let his nephew down.

Not now. Not ever.

He was nothing like his father, and he'd prove it to his dying day if he had to.

If he had to, he'd even go to his father's parole hearing in February and deliver his victim impact statement in person, although it was the last thing in the world he wanted to do. He hadn't seen the man in eleven years and had no desire to see him ever again, but if that's what it would take to keep his father behind bars and away from him and Aiden, he'd do it in a heartbeat.

Some sins were too big to be forgiven. And Steve didn't want Aiden to pay for that man's sins the way Steve himself had paid—and continued to pay.

In the backyard, Chloe chewed her lip, something close to compassion in her eyes. "Have you interviewed anyone else?"

"Aunt Mabel said there's only been one person who's replied to the job posting so far." He paused. "You."

She nodded and stared off into space for a second, crossing her arms over her chest. "I'm moving to Boston after Christmas."

"Okay…"

She turned those expressive eyes of hers on him. "So this wouldn't be a long-term thing."

Steve hadn't been aware that his shoulders were tight, but he felt them loosen in relief. "Temporary is fine. Even if we can't find another nanny, he'll be old enough for daycare in the new year. I just really need to get back to work, and as I'm sure you can see, my great-aunt's in no condition to watch a baby."

Chloe gave him a determined little nod. "All right. When do you want me to start?"

He shifted Aiden so he could take a quick glance at his watch. "How about now?"

Chapter Two

Chloe stared at the front door of the cottage on Frog Pond as it shut behind Steve, feeling shell-shocked. He'd been clumsy as a teen—tall and lanky with big hands and feet, and arms and legs that stretched like saltwater taffy—but he'd grown into himself since then.

Now he had broad shoulders and was lean without being skinny, muscled without having too much bulk. He'd been wearing pressed gray pants and a blue button-down shirt open at the neck, probably because he'd been coming from some sort of meeting at the bank.

With his blue eyes, strong jaw and short, golden-brown hair, the man was definitely easy on the eyes. And if Chloe hadn't already known better, she'd have thought he was nice, too—the way he'd assured her that the formula mishap wasn't her fault, the way he so obviously cared about Aiden and Mabel.

But nice guys didn't kiss high school girls who were two years their junior and then fall off the face of the earth.

Good-looking isn't the same as a good character. If her ex-boyfriend, Dan, had taught her anything, it was that physical attraction was worth about as much as a piece of penny candy. So, Chloe could take all those pitter-patters she'd been experiencing around Steve and lock them in the closet. She wasn't going to act on her romantic feelings for him ever again.

Aiden gave a little peep and she lowered him from her shoulder. His clothes were still damp from the formula spill, and his skin was sticky. "We should get you cleaned up, shouldn't we?" she said.

The baby made a funny sound and yawned, his little face scrunching as his mouth opened. With his big, cartoon-like eyes and his tiny pointed chin, he was just too adorable.

Steve had dropped them off at his waterside cottage on Frog Pond before heading to his clinic, and it was a surprisingly nice home. The kitchen and bathroom had clearly been updated—they both had granite counters and newly tiled floors. The family room was open to the kitchen, and it had a sliding-glass door that led out to a large back deck with a fantastic view of Frog Pond.

The pond itself was calm and smallish, hemmed in by a combination of pitch pine and oak trees that were mostly barren this time of year. Floating in the middle of the freshwater pond was an old wooden dock that the neighborhood kids swam out to and sunbathed on during the summer. Chloe herself had swum out there a few times over the years.

The vibe on Frog Pond was more insular and self-contained than it was elsewhere on Cape Cod, where the ocean stretched to infinity and the sky seemed boundless. Here, it felt cozier. Quieter.

Chloe liked the quiet. It sounded cheesy, but she felt closer to her parents in the quiet. Closer to God.

Although Steve didn't have any Christmas decorations inside the house, there were several trees out back he'd bedecked with colorful lights, which made Chloe happy. Christmas had been a bit of a struggle for her since the car crash that had hurt her back and killed her parents, but she was determined to make this her best Christmas yet. After all, who knew where she'd end up getting a job after her student teaching internship was over? This might be her last-ever Christmas on Cape Cod.

Her best friend, Laura, and her fiancé, Jonathan, were hosting a big community potluck at

The Sea Glass Inn following the Christmas pageant at church on Christmas Eve, and Chloe was helping them plan the whole thing. In fact, they were meeting for brunch tomorrow morning so they could discuss the menu and the musical entertainment. Chloe was in charge of picking the music for the caroling, and she could hardly wait.

Humming "O Come, All Ye Faithful," she carried the baby into the bathroom and filled the little blue baby tub with lukewarm water before taking off Aiden's dirty clothes. She put him in the tub, her left hand cradling his head, her right hand wielding a wet washcloth and wiping him down.

When she'd finished cleaning him up, she swaddled him in a thick, fluffy towel and took him into his nursery, which could have been ripped out of the pages of a parenting magazine, it was so well done. It had baby-blue walls and a fantastically detailed Noah's Ark mural painted on the wall behind the crib. There were also books and toys, and an intricate animal mobile to keep him entertained while he lay in bed.

She wondered how much of this had been Steve's doing, and how much of it had been his sister's. It was a beautiful room.

She saw his sister's bedroom, too, half packed

into boxes. How sad for all of them, to lose her so suddenly, and so young.

In the nursery, she proceeded to diaper Aiden and get him dressed. She laughed in disbelief when she saw that his wardrobe consisted of twelve identical white onesies and twelve identical pairs of white footie pajamas. Steve was clearly one of those guys who didn't care about clothing. Chloe would have to remedy the situation. Stat.

How cute would the baby look dressed up like a little Christmas elf?

She poked around to see if she could find a stroller or a baby carrier but came up empty. She'd have to remedy that, too. With the way her back had been acting up lately, she wouldn't be able to carry Aiden on her shoulder for any extended period of time.

Herniated disks would do that to a person, even if they'd healed a lot since the crash.

She gave Aiden another bottle. He fell asleep at the end of his feed, and she was able to place him, sleeping, in the travel crib in the family room. While he slept, she poked around some more. Steve's fridge was stocked with a few cans of Sprite, some milk and a half-empty carton of eggnog. The freezer held a handful of burritos, a pizza, and an unopened bag of corn. The counter was lined with dirty dishes.

Chloe microwaved herself a frozen burrito for dinner—Steve had asked her if she'd be willing to watch the baby while he stayed late at work—and then got started on the dishes.

Her brother might call her a people pleaser, but if she was going to work for this guy for even a few weeks, she might as well make herself useful.

Steve didn't pull into his driveway until a little after eight o'clock at night. He'd been going over his books. Although his business loan was brand-new, thanks to the unexpected expenses associated with Eloise's funeral and the fact that he'd had to cancel two weeks' worth of client appointments, he was worried he was going to miss his first payment.

He'd been at the bank earlier to see if he could take out a personal loan on top of his business loan. The down payment on Family Physio had wiped out his savings, and he'd been forced to put Eloise's funeral expenses on his credit card. He suspected there'd be costs associated with her hospital stay, too. He just wasn't sure yet how expensive those charges would turn out to be.

He pressed the heels of his hands to his eyes. The clinic's cash flow was good, and if things had gone smoothly, he would have been able to earn back his investment within three or four years. After that, the profits would have been gravy.

When he and Eloise had been sketching everything out, it had seemed like such a solid plan. She'd get to stay home with the baby, and he'd be able to give Aiden everything he and Eloise had lacked when they were growing up. Stability. Financial security. Fatherly love.

Given that he was never going to get married, it had seemed like the closest he'd ever get to having a family of his own.

But God had had other plans.

His sister was dead and the bank had turned him down for the personal loan. Which meant the interest he'd have to pay on his credit card if he couldn't quickly pay down all his debt would be astronomical.

This really wasn't good. And now he'd have to pay Chloe's salary on top of all the other expenses. But what else could he do? If he couldn't work, he couldn't even dream of paying off what he owed.

At least he'd be able to reschedule all those canceled appointments now that he had a nanny in place for Aiden. That was a blessing, and he was definitely grateful.

He took a moment to do a deep breathing exercise to try to dispel some of the anxiety that was buzzing around his stomach. It helped a bit, but not that much.

Getting out of the car, he listened to the night sounds around him. The wind in the trees, the hoot of an owl, the pond's anemic waves lapping the small shore. Some people thought it was odd to come to Cape Cod and choose to live next to a pond rather than the ocean, but Steve liked it. He found it soothing. And the Christmas lights he'd put in the trees made him smile.

He hadn't been sure he'd have the heart to celebrate this year, but he wanted to make Aiden's first Christmas special, even if the boy wouldn't actually remember it. Focusing on his nephew, rather than the loss of his sister, made it easier to go on.

His were the only lights to be seen, since most of the people who owned houses around Frog Pond and its freshwater beach used them as summer homes only. His reclusive grandfather, who'd left this place to him and Eloise, had lived here full-time after his retirement, putting up with Steve's visit the summer he was seventeen only because Steve had promised to be quiet and stay out of the old man's way.

Since his granddad's death five years earlier, the small, cedar-shingled cottage had sat vacant. Eloise had made noises about selling it a few times over the years, but Steve had been well aware that she'd take her share of the money and spend it on drugs and alcohol, so he'd always said no. After she went to rehab, it had seemed like the perfect place for her to focus on her recovery and raise the baby.

And because he hadn't been able to protect her from what had happened with their parents, he'd wanted to be there for her as she started this new chapter in her life.

For all the good that had done.

But he wasn't going to start feeling sorry for himself now.

Inside, Steve found Chloe asleep on the couch, Aiden snoozing in the travel crib nearby. Chloe was curled up with her head propped on the armrest, her mascara smudged, her hair a little mussed, some spit-up on her sleeve. Oddly, seeing her like that, her features soft with sleep, made him feel calmer than he'd felt all day— maybe even since Eloise had died.

He felt an unfamiliar pang of longing in his chest. Coming to Cape Cod the summer he was seventeen had been a respite—a haven from the chaos at home. And Chloe? She'd been a huge part of making it feel that way.

What if...?

He squashed that thought before it had time to take hold. A guy wouldn't get a second chance with a girl like Chloe. Especially not a guy like him.

He crouched next to the arm of the sofa and

put his hand on her shoulder, the faux fur trim on her red sweater tickling his fingers. "Chloe," he said in a low voice.

She snorted and sat up with a start. "I'm sorry. Did I fall asleep?"

She looked so alarmed it made him smile. "Just a little." He tipped his head in Aiden's direction. "How long has he been out?"

Squinting at the clock on his microwave, which was visible from the sofa, she said, "Forty-five minutes?"

"How'd everything go?"

"It was fine. I hope you don't mind that I fell asleep." She gave him a sheepish look. "Newborns are exhausting."

He felt the corner of his mouth quirk up. She was cute when she was embarrassed. "Tell me about it."

She stood and picked up her purse. "So, I'll see you Monday, I guess?"

He straightened and nodded. "Monday it is." Then he rubbed the back of his neck. "And thanks again, Blondie. I appreciate your willingness to help us out."

Waving off his gratitude, she said, "As long as you pay me for my time, Weston, it's all good." She moved toward the front door, slipped on her shoes, then stopped abruptly. "Oh, wait. My car—"

He snatched his keys out of his pocket. She'd walked to his great-aunt's house for the interview, and he'd driven them all straight here. "Take mine."

She gave him an odd look. "You want me to take your car? Overnight?"

He glanced at the travel crib. "I'd offer to drive you home but…" He spread his hands, his lips curving up once again. "You know what they say about sleeping babies."

She still had that odd, vaguely incredulous look on her face. "I can call a cab."

He held his keys out again, shaking them a little. "Take my car. It's fine. You can bring it back in the morning."

Her eyebrows pinched together. "Tomorrow's Saturday."

"You got other plans?"

She looked at him for a long moment, then something inside her seemed to shift and give in. "I'm having brunch with friends, but I can stop by after."

"Bring it back when you're done, and then Aiden and I will drop you off at home."

She gave him another long look, as though she couldn't quite figure him out. "You're a very trusting person."

He shrugged. "Aunt Mabel clearly thinks you're an upstanding citizen," he said, because he and his great-aunt had had a few minutes to debrief before he'd brought Chloe to his house. "And anyway," he added, trying to keep a straight face while he said it, "she told me where you live."

Chloe's eyes went wide. "She did?"

"You live above The Candy Shack with the seventy-year-old proprietor of the store as your roommate. How can you not lead with that in every conversation you have?"

She laughed, and a sense of warmth spread through him. He liked the sound of her laugh. It was like the trill of a flute, or tinkling bells.

"Seriously," he said. "Every boyhood dream I had about living in a chocolate factory is springing to life right now."

She laughed again. "I don't live *in* the store, you know."

"But it must smell great up there, doesn't it? Where does Irene make the fudge? In your apartment? Or in the store?"

She kept laughing. "You're as bad as Jonathan!"

"Jonathan?" he asked, the sense of warmth receding. He should have assumed she had a boyfriend. Maybe she was even married, although she wasn't wearing a ring.

"Remember my friend, Laura, from church camp?"

He shook his head. He didn't. The only girl he remembered from church camp that summer was her.

For weeks, he'd looked for excuses to stand next to her, to sit beside her, to hear her laugh. When she'd finally noticed him, he'd had to content himself with holding her hand when they were out in a group, because she'd been young—only fifteen—and her parents wouldn't let her go out on a date with a boy alone.

And then he'd kissed her that last night, right before he went home to New Hampshire and all the terrible, awful things had happened with his dad.

"Jonathan's her fiancé."

"Got it," he said, feeling relieved, although none of his reasons for failing to pursue a relationship with her—or anyone, aside from his one, short-lived attempt in college—had changed over the years. "Hey, what's your brother up to these days?"

"Brett? He took over the family restaurant."

"Oh, nice," he said, with some surprise. "I thought he wanted to join the navy."

"He did that, too. Just one tour, though."

"Wow. Good for him."

Aiden made a noise and Chloe held up Steve's keys. "Well, I should get going."

"Thanks again," he said. "You're a lifesaver. For real."

She smirked and gave him a funny little bow with a hand flourish—she'd always been quirky like that—and then she was out the door.

Chapter Three

The next morning, Chloe stopped at The Barnacle Bakery on Main Street to pick up some pastries for brunch at The Sea Glass Inn. The restaurant was decorated to the nines, with Christmas lights and colorful ornaments hanging from the rafters, and tiny poinsettia plants placed in the center of each table, almost all of which were full.

Pastor Nate, his dad, Bill, and his preteen son, Hayden, were sitting in a booth by the front window, finishing up plates of bacon, eggs and hash browns. "Chloe!" Bill called out when he saw her. "How's that lovely roommate of yours?"

"Irene's great, Bill," Chloe said, grinning. She'd long suspected that the pastor's dad, a distinguished older gentleman who went to the gym five days a week and volunteered as the chess coach at the local high school in his spare time, had a soft spot for Irene. Her septuagenarian roommate, however, always brushed off Chloe's teasing with a quelling look and a prim fluff of her hair. "He's only sixty-five, young lady. Way too young for me!"

"You should stop by The Candy Shack later," Chloe added. "She's making gingerbread fudge."

Hayden sat straight at the mention of the Christmas-flavored fudge and pushed his glasses up on his nose. "Can we go, Grandpa?"

"If it's okay with your dad," Bill said, nodding his chin at Nate.

"Sure, Hayden," the pastor said, setting down his cup of coffee, his wedding ring flashing in the light. His wife had been gone since before he and Hayden had moved to Wychmere Bay, but he never took it off. "You and Grandpa can go get some fudge this afternoon while I'm at work."

"Yes!" Hayden clenched his fist in victory, then had to straighten his glasses again. Chloe gave him a fist bump before raising her hand in a farewell wave.

"I'll see you gents later," she said, backing away. "Got to pick up some donuts for brunch at The Sea Glass Inn."

"Have fun," Nate said.

"Tell Irene I send my regards," Bill added.

Chloe smiled and nodded. Irene was definitely going to hear all about this little encounter later today.

After choosing a selection of eggnog-, peppermint mocha-and pumpkin-spice-flavored pastries—and throwing in a chocolate-frosted Rudolph donut with pretzel pieces for the antlers just for five-year-old Emma—Chloe carefully set the box on the floor of Steve's car and drove to The Sea Glass Inn.

Pulling into a parking space out front, she marveled over the transformation Laura and Jonathan had pulled off since Thanksgiving. With its cedar shingles and black shutters, the beachfront inn always looked stately, but now it almost looked like a gingerbread house, with a lush green garland framing the front door, wreaths hanging from all nine of the front windows, and a veritable herd of light-up reindeers grazing in the yard.

There hadn't been a white Christmas on Cape Cod for the last two years, but Chloe hoped the weather would oblige this time around. How warm and welcoming would the inn look with all these lights and greenery *and* a fine dusting of snow?

"Aunt Chloe! Aunt Chloe!" Laura's daughter, Emma, yelled as she ran outside to greet her, wearing red pants, no shoes and a sweatshirt with little Santa hats all over it. "We putted up our Chwistmas twee!"

"You did?" Chloe set the box of donuts on the roof of Steve's car and crouched to give the green-eyed girl a hug. "Amazing!"

Emma flung herself into Chloe's open arms. "And we're going to bake cookies and sing songs and have a big, yummy dinner on Chwistmas Eve!"

"We sure are!" Chloe agreed. "But come on, silly, it's chilly out and you're not wearing a jacket." She arched an eyebrow. "Or shoes."

Emma giggled as Chloe led her inside the inn, which had that wonderful Christmassy pine-tree smell thanks to the giant Christmas tree standing in front of the plate-glass windows in the parlor. Wrapped in twinkly white lights, hung with big red bows and strung with generous strands of popcorn and cranberries, it looked like something out of an old-time movie.

"I putted the star on top!" Emma announced proudly. "Mr. Jonafin held me up!"

"Wow, good job!"

"Emma!" Laura exclaimed, coming through the swinging door from the dining room with her hands on her hips. "You know better than to run outside without shoes or a jacket!"

"Sowwy, Mommy," the girl said. "I saw Aunt

Chloe get out of the car wif a box of donuts and I was too excited to wait!"

"Go put on some socks so you're ready the next time you need shoes, please."

As Emma scurried off, Chloe unzipped her puffy pink jacket and hung it on the coatrack by the door. "The decorations look great."

"Don't they? We spent all last weekend putting them up."

"Sorry I wasn't here to help."

"How'd the apartment hunting go?" her friend asked.

Chloe grimaced. "Boston's so expensive."

"Nothing? Still?"

"Well," Chloe said, "there was one place. I thought it might be too much, but now that I've got a nannying gig for the next few weeks, I think I'll be able to swing it."

Laura's eyes popped. "Wait. You got a nannying gig? Since when?"

"Since yesterday."

"For who?"

Chloe was definitely *not* looking forward to answering that question. The summer she'd met Steve had also been the summer she'd met Laura. And she had no doubt that her friend had some very vivid memories of the embarrassing extent of Chloe's teenage crush on Steve. "Did you know Mabel has a great-nephew?"

"Is he local?" Laura asked, tucking a strand of her long brown hair behind her ear.

"He is now."

"Have I met him?"

Chloe bit her lip. "Uh, you *have* met him, but it was a long time ago…"

Laura scrunched her nose. "Who is it?"

"Remember Steve Weston?"

Laura's mouth dropped open. "No!"

"Yes."

"You're nannying for *Steve Weston*?"

Chloe shrugged. "I didn't know it was him when I applied for the job, but whatever."

"Whatever?" Laura gaped at her. "After all the anguish you went through over that guy, all you have to say for yourself is *whatever*?"

Chloe shrugged again. She'd taken his rejection hard, but knowing what she knew now, she suspected that her intense and overwhelming reaction had been less about what had actually happened and more about her then undiagnosed—and untreated—depression.

According to the therapist she'd started seeing after her parents died, normal teenage heartbreak lasted a couple of weeks. It didn't stretch out for months. It didn't lead people to stop talking to their friends and skip school events. It didn't lead them to sleep all hours of the day and stay up all night crying and feeling worthless.

As a teen, she hadn't known enough to label her experience as clinical depression. Instead, she'd thought the problem was unrequited love.

Eventually, the dark feelings had receded, and Chloe had gone back to her old self. But until she'd started seeing the therapist, there had always been a piece of her that was terrified that if she let herself have feelings for someone who didn't reciprocate them again, she'd be opening the door to that same kind of all-consuming despair.

As a result, she hadn't dated anyone else in high school, keeping all the boys at arm's length. And after high school? She'd tried...a little. But her fear meant that—until her therapist had explained to her what depression was, how it worked and how to treat it—nothing ever seemed to progress beyond one or two dates.

Until Dan, of course.

Which was a whole other headache.

Chloe sighed. She'd never talked about her depression with anyone besides her therapist—not her brother, not Irene, and not even her best friend. They were obviously aware that she'd gone through a hard time after her parents died, but her diagnosis was personal, it was private, and honestly? She didn't want them to see her differently, or to think they had to handle her with kid gloves.

Answering Laura's question, she said, "That was a long time ago, Laura. We were just kids."

Laura goggled her eyes and stared at Chloe for a long moment. Then, slowly, she said, "So, he's married now? He has children?"

Chloe shook her head. "His sister died. He's caring for his nephew."

Laura got a glint in her eyes that Chloe didn't like one bit. "And what did he say when you asked why he never called you after that kiss?"

"I'm not asking him that!" Chloe shot back, horrified at the very idea of having that conversation with Steve. It was embarrassing to think about how starry-eyed she'd been, how hopeful. How sure she'd been that he was going to call or text her. How crushed she'd been when he hadn't followed through.

"Why not?"

"Because it's desperate. It implies I've been thinking about it—thinking about *him*—all this time."

"Well," Laura said, lifting an eyebrow, "haven't you?"

"Laura…" Chloe groaned. "I have not been pining away for Steve Weston for the last eleven years. You know that."

"I know. But it's interesting timing, isn't it? Given what just happened with you know who," Laura said, obviously referring to Dan.

Chloe groaned again. Maybe she *wouldn't* give Irene a hard time about Bill Anderson anymore. This was excruciating.

"What?" Laura asked innocently.

"Don't do that."

"Do what?"

"Don't play innocent with me, missy," Chloe said, shaking her finger at her friend.

Laura laughed. "I think you've been living with Irene too long."

"And *I* think you're trying to invent something between me and Steve Weston that's just not there."

Laura steepled her fingers, that maddening glint still in her eye. "And what, pray tell, would I be inventing?"

Chloe shook her head in irritation. "You're acting like I still have feelings for him, after all this time."

"Do you still have feelings for him, after all this time?"

"Absolutely not!"

"Hear me out. First love is a powerful thi—"

"I was not in love with Steve Weston! I was in like. That's all. Some sad little version of puppy like."

"I don't know, sweetie—" Laura started.

Chloe cut her off. "Well, I do. I wasn't in love with him then, and I'm not in danger of falling in love with him now. The baby needs a nanny and I need some cash so I can start my student teaching placement without having to worry about the cost of living in Boston. That's all this is about."

Laura gave her one more sideways glance, then sighed and said, "Since when did you decide you wanted to be a nanny?"

Chloe snorted. "Since yesterday afternoon when Mabel told me her great-nephew was willing to pay good money for my services."

"Is he cute?"

Chloe rolled her eyes. "Didn't we just talk about this?"

"The baby, Chlo! Is the *baby* cute?"

Chloe let out a relieved breath. The truth was that she thought Steve was more than cute, but she wasn't about to admit that to Laura. "Oh, ha, ha. Yeah, he's adorable."

"I can't even remember when Emma was that small."

"Have you and your fiancé talked about having more children?" Chloe asked with a teasing grin. Laura had just gotten engaged in September, and the woman was over the moon.

Laura's eyes filled with humor. "Of course. Jonathan says he wants, like, five or six of them."

"Whoa. Seriously?"

Laura laughed. "We'll see. But he's already contacted a lawyer about adopting Emma."

"Really?" Chloe said, happy for her friend, whose ex-husband had abandoned her while she was pregnant and never pursued much of a relationship with his daughter. "That's so awesome."

"I know. I can hardly believe it. We're so blessed."

"Jonathan's the one who's blessed," Chloe insisted. "You're a catch, sister."

"Why, thank you. So are you." She looped her arm through Chloe's. "Now let's go track down Emma before the boys get here. She's been upstairs long enough that I'm sure she's torn her room apart."

When Chloe showed up a little after eleven, Steve was unshowered, unshaven, and about to lose his mind.

He had the baby up on his shoulder, screaming into his ear. Chloe took one look at them and immediately held out her hands. "Here, give him to me."

He handed Aiden over and then brushed a hand through his hair, aware that it was sticking up at all kinds of bizarro angles. The baby cried louder. Steve shot her an apologetic look. "He's been really fussy."

She held Aiden carefully on her shoulder, supporting his head, and bounced him up and down a little. "Big adjustment, being out in the big, bad world. Of course he's a little out of sorts."

"If you don't mind watching him for a few minutes, I'll go clean up and then we can drop you off."

"You know what, Weston? Go get some sleep. I'm okay to hang around for a couple hours."

"Really? I don't want to impose…"

She gave him a half smile. "It's no trouble. Really. And I brought one of those baby wrap carriers. I'll take him out for a walk so you can get some sleep. Hold him for a second and I'll put it on."

He took the baby back, almost unable to believe what she was offering, and she reached into her giant shoulder bag and plucked out a long, colorful piece of fabric. Then she twisted it around her body until she'd made a little pouch in the front, like a mama kangaroo.

"Here," she said, holding her hands out for Aiden. Steve gave her the baby and watched as she carefully inserted him into the pouch, his little body snug against her chest, his head cradled between her collarbone and one of the soft, wide straps. Almost as soon as Aiden was settled into the carrier, he stopped crying.

"Is that thing safe?" Steve asked with some concern. "He's not going to fall out?"

Chloe gave him a look of exaggerated patience. "No, Weston. He's not going to fall out. You want to feel it?" she asked, gesturing toward the fabric. "It's perfectly secure."

Steve placed his hand on the baby's fabric-covered back, trying not to notice just how close he was standing to Chloe, whose beautiful blond hair smelled like vanilla and spun sugar, and trying not to wonder how it would feel, all these years later, to have her back in his arms.

You burned that bridge a long time ago, buddy. Don't even go there.

He refocused his attention on the baby. The wrap was definitely not loose, and Aiden seemed to be snug.

"I did some research on the best baby carriers after I got home last night. This one got top grades, and it was in stock at The Baby Boutique," she said, naming a store on Main Street. "My friend Laura and I walked over there after brunch."

He was touched that she'd been thinking about Aiden after hours, but he didn't want her spending her own money on baby gear. He rubbed the back of his neck. "How much did you spend? I'll reimburse you," he said, even though the thought of spending more money right now made him feel sick.

She waved a hand. "Don't worry about it. Just go. Get some sleep. You look like you need it."

Ashamed at the relief he felt that she didn't want to be repaid, he nodded. "Are you sure you don't have anywhere else you need to be?"

She shook her head. "I'm all yours."

Although he knew exactly what she did—and didn't—mean, her words did something to him. Cracked something open inside him. Made him wonder what it would be like to have a person of his own.

"You fall asleep on your feet there, Weston?" Chloe was looking at him funny. He must have been staring.

And why did she keep calling him by his last name? She'd never done that back in the day. But maybe that was her way of keeping her distance, letting him know that even though she worked for him and was taking care of his nephew, she wasn't his friend.

Which was just as it should be. He couldn't afford to get all nostalgic about her, anyway. He had to focus on keeping his head—and his business—above water.

"Sorry," he said. "If you're sure you don't mind, I really *am* tired."

She peered up at him through those overgrown bangs of hers. "I'm sure."

He went to his bedroom, pulled the curtains shut and almost immediately fell into a deep, dreamless sleep.

When he woke up, it was almost three o'clock in the afternoon. He shot up. Four hours had passed! Had Chloe been walking Aiden around the pond this whole time? Had something happened?

He jumped out of bed and poked his head into the nursery. Nothing. No one in the family room, either. He was about to call her cell phone when he looked onto the deck and saw her sitting at his patio table, calmly giving Aiden a bottle. He shoved his feet into an old pair of tennis shoes and went outside to join them, rubbing his arms against the chill.

Chloe looked up and smiled as he slid the glass door closed. "Rip Van Winkle has risen. How're you feeling?"

Steve rubbed his eyes and sat across from her. "Better. You must be a baby whisperer. How did you keep him quiet for so long?"

"He likes the wrap. Apparently, it makes babies feel safe and secure. He conked out when I was halfway around the pond. He slept for almost two hours. I sat out here on the deck for most of it and read a book."

He sat back in his chair, feeling relieved. "You're a genius. I think I only got, like, one or two hours of sleep last night. He just cried and cried."

"I'll show you how to put on the wrap if you want."

"Guys can use it, too?"

She snorted. "Of course."

"You're a genius," he said again.

She pointed her chin toward an empty bowl on the table. "I had some cereal. I hope you don't mind."

He shook his head. "Help yourself to whatever you want. Sorry I didn't show you where everything is."

"I poked around a little."

He nodded and went inside. After he got dressed in gray cargo pants and a rugby shirt, he found Chloe and the baby in the nursery. Aiden was lying on the play mat Steve had bought for him, a colorful, jungle-themed piece of equipment with a mirror and a bunch of little rattles hanging from the bars. Chloe was lying next to him on her stomach, pointing to the different animals and telling Aiden what they were.

"This is a lion. He goes 'rawwwr.' He has yellow fur and a big mane around his neck. He can run really fast." In her ripped jeans and well-worn Boston Bruins sweatshirt, she looked relaxed, happy and very young.

He stood in the doorway for a minute, watching them. He liked the way Chloe touched Aiden's head, stomach and feet when she was talking to him. She was really great with him. He could tell she was going to do a fantastic job.

Standing there, Steve felt a fierce yearning to be the kind of man she could look at the way she was looking at the baby right now—with joy and affection in her eyes. He wasn't that man, though. He'd never be that man. His father's actions had made sure of that.

"So, how long have you been nannying?" he asked, leaning against the doorjamb. She sat up, her hand resting lightly on Aiden's stomach, and looked at him, those long bangs of hers falling into her big brown eyes.

"Hmm, let's see." She stroked her chin, as though giving his question great consideration. "This would be day two."

He laughed, then realized she was serious. "Really? But I thought…"

"Mabel would want to hire a professional?" she asked, the hint of a smile playing on her lips. "Guess not."

"So, why…?"

She shrugged. "I like kids. I used to babysit a lot when I was younger. And it seemed like a good way to earn some extra money while the restaurant's closed."

"Why's the restaurant closed?"

"We're renovating."

"Ah."

"I won't be working there anymore, though, even when the reno's finished," she said. "I'm almost done with my teaching degree."

Well, that made her decision to become Aiden's nanny make a little more sense. "You really *do* like kids."

She smiled. "I really do."

"What do you want to teach?"

"The little ones. Kindergarten or first grade."

"Nice."

"And you?" she asked, waggling a toy in front of Aiden. "I heard you bought Family Physio."

He nodded. "I did."

"That's cool."

"Yeah, it's a challenge. I'm used to the clinical side of things. The business side? Not so much."

"You were always smart, though. I'm sure you'll pick it up quickly."

He couldn't help it—he smiled, her words making him feel warm inside. "Let's hope so. Had to take out a big loan to buy it."

She made a face. "I know how that goes. Even though I've been taking classes online, tuition's still expensive."

"So…why the move to Boston? Cost of living there is pretty steep."

"Oh, you know," she said vaguely, looking away. "Fresh start, change of pace, yadda yadda yadda."

"Sure," he replied, sensing there was more to the story but not wanting to push. "Same thing with me and my sister, coming here."

She leaned back on her hands and tipped up her face. "Did you ever come back here again? You know, after that summer?"

He frowned, wondering if she was going to demand an explanation for why he'd never called her. Wondering, if she did, what it was that he'd say.

Because he couldn't tell her the truth. He knew he was being a coward again, but if he told her and she couldn't handle it, what would he do with the baby? He had to get back to work, or else he was going to lose the clinic. He couldn't afford for her to walk out on him and Aiden now.

"Just once, when my grandfather died," he answered carefully.

"That was a few years ago, wasn't it?"

He nodded. "Five years ago."

"What brought you back now?"

He sighed and rubbed the back of his neck. "Did Aunt Mabel tell you much about my sister?"

"A little," she said. "I'm really sorry for your loss."

"Thanks." He gave her a sad smile. "She had a drinking problem. Like my parents. When she got pregnant, she went to rehab, and when she got out, both of us thought it would be best to raise the baby somewhere quiet, with a slower pace of life."

Her eyes widened. "You were going to raise him together?"

He shifted uncomfortably. He knew that people didn't always understand his relationship with Eloise. "She was my sister. She needed help."

"Wow, that's…" She trailed off.

"She'd been through a lot, Chloe. You have no idea."

She looked away, pulling at a stray piece of thread on her sweatshirt. "You don't have to explain yourself to me."

Aiden waved his hands in the air, all herky-jerky, and let out a cry. Chloe gave a little chuckle. "I think someone needs a diaper change."

Steve pushed himself off the doorjamb and stooped down to pick up the baby. "Let's get you changed, buddy," Steve told him, "and then we're going to figure out how to use that baby wrap."

Chapter Four

"Uh, are you sure this is how it works?" Steve asked, holding out his arms, the fabric of the baby wrap draped over his shoulders and hanging down like wings.

Chloe was sitting at his little kitchen table, sunlight streaming in, Aiden in her arms. She tried to hold back her laughter as she watched Steve standing in the middle of his family room looking so perplexed. "Yes, just cross the front pieces—yeah, like that—and tuck them under the piece of fabric at your waist."

"Like this?" he asked skeptically, following her directions.

"Just like that."

He looked up. "Now what?"

"Now wrap them around your waist."

His eyebrows furled together. "Again?"

"Again," she confirmed. He wrapped the fab-

ric around his waist as instructed. "And now tie
it in a double knot in the front."

"And that's supposed to hold him?"

"Unless you're really bad at tying knots," she
said, lips twitching.

He gave her a look of mild exasperation. "I
was a Boy Scout, I'll have you know."

She smirked. "Then you shouldn't have any
problems."

"I just…" He still looked confused, and a little worried. "Are you sure it's not going to fall
apart?"

"I walked all the way around Frog Pond with
him in the carrier this morning. I promise you,
it'll hold him." She stood and moved closer to
him, holding the baby. "Just pull the front panel
out so we can slide him in."

He looked down at the wrap. "What front
panel?"

"You can put him in on either side. Just decide which side you want him on, and pull the
fabric away from your shoulder."

"Like this?"

She stepped even closer. "Perfect." She ma-
neuvered Aiden so he slid, feetfirst, into the
pouch of fabric on Steve's chest and abdomen.

"Whoa. Neat," Steve said, giving Aiden a few
gentle pats through the cloth.

"Walk around a little. Get a feel for it."

He took a tour of the family room, then went out onto his big back deck. Chloe trailed along behind him, and he looked at her over his shoulder. "Is this what it feels like to be pregnant?"

"Couldn't tell ya, Weston. No frame of reference."

"I bet this is kind of what it feels like, at least from a center-of-gravity point of view."

Chloe gave a noncommittal shrug. "Maybe."

"Did you know that male seahorses are the ones who give birth, not the females? They're practically the only animals on earth that have such a thing as male pregnancy."

"Okay…"

"Well, them and sea dragons."

She felt her eyebrows go up. "Sea dragons?"

"Look them up. They're little. And cool."

"Did you want to be a marine biologist when you grew up?"

The corner of his mouth quirked up. "I just think they're interesting, that's all."

He did another circle around the deck. "So, this is fun," he said, lifting his hands off Aiden's back. "Look, Ma! No hands!"

Chloe tried not to laugh. She remembered this about him, from that summer at church camp—the boyish enthusiasm. She was glad he still had it. It was entertaining.

He adjusted the way the wrap was sitting on

his shoulder. "Well, thanks for showing me how to put on the carrier. I like it. I can tell it's going to come in handy."

She smiled. "You're welcome. Just don't fall asleep with him in it. You could roll over and smother him."

He made an *eek* face, his eyes looking even bluer under the blue sky than they normally did. "Duly noted."

Her phone rang and she took it out of her back pocket and checked the display. Pastor Nate. He probably needed to discuss the music for the Christmas pageant, or to find someone to fill in on the piano tomorrow during one of the services. She glanced up at Steve. "I have to take this. Hold on a sec."

He drifted away from her, back into the house. She took the call, discovering that Nate did, indeed, want her to fill in on the piano during tomorrow's church service. Chloe loved playing, so of course she agreed.

After she hung up, she went inside. Steve had taken Aiden out of the wrap and was drinking a big glass of water. "So, we should get you home, huh?"

"Sounds good," she said.

As they backed out of his driveway, he flicked a glance at her and asked, "Everything okay with your call?"

"Oh, yeah. It was just my pastor calling. He needs someone to play the piano tomorrow at church."

He gave her another quick look. "I knew you were a good singer, but the piano, too, huh? What other surprises do you have up your sleeve? Flute? Trombone? Kazoo?"

She smirked. "Kazoo? Really?"

He grinned. "Only instrument I could ever play."

"If you can hum, you can play the kazoo."

"Exactly." He nodded with satisfaction. "So… don't leave me hanging. Drums? Xylophone? Electric violin?"

She laughed. "Close. Piano and acoustic guitar."

"Really?" He sounded surprised. "How come you never played guitar for us back in the day?"

A few of the boys at church camp had brought their guitars to the bonfires, sometimes for background music, sometimes so everyone could sing along.

She shrugged. "Shy, I guess." It was true—that summer had been the first time she'd been out in mixed company. Before then, it had just been her and her girlfriends, going to movies together, going to the local clam shack, going to the mall.

"I can see it, though," Steve said. "You've got stage presence."

She laughed again. "How would you know? You've never seen me play."

"Yeah, but you still go to Wychmere Community Church, don't you?" he asked, making her wonder why she hadn't seen him there since he'd been back. "I'll come watch you play tomorrow, and then I can tell you for sure." He grinned. "Besides, all those wild clothes you used to wear kinda screamed 'rock star.'"

She snorted. "Rock star?"

He hitched a shoulder. "Or, I don't know, singer-songwriter, at least. You were always a bit…fashion-y."

She was trying hard not to burst out laughing again. "Fashion-y?"

"All those old clothes you'd find at the thrift store."

"You remember that?"

He gave her an amused, sideways glance. "Of course I remember it, Blondie. I liked them. You were unique."

She felt her cheeks heat. Was she *blushing* because Steve Weston said he'd liked her zany teenage fashion sense?

The couple of times she'd worn a thrift store outfit in front of Dan, he'd wrinkled his nose and told her to change. Actually, he'd frequently told her to change her clothes before they went out. And fix her hair. And put on high heels. And reapply her makeup.

No matter how refreshing Steve's comments might be, she needed to get a handle on herself and her blushing, fast. Just because he was a good-looking guy who was sweet to the baby did *not* mean she was going to fall at his feet all over again.

She knew how that story ended. And it hadn't been fun.

He took a left onto Main Street, which had shiny tinsel Christmas tree decorations affixed to all the lampposts, and she said, "Okay, then. Pull over."

"Uh…what?"

"You heard me. Pull over."

"Okay…" He pulled up next to a parking meter. "What's going on? Did I offend you or something?"

She opened her door. "Nope. We're going to get Aiden some new clothes."

His brow furrowed in confusion. "What's wrong with the clothes he has?"

"You can't just buy him a bunch of the same outfits—all those little white onesies and pajamas. It's weird."

Steve's lips twitched. "Weird?"

She threw her hands in the air. "Yeah, it's odd

to dress him in the same thing all the time. Like some strange little uniform."

He shrugged, but there was a smile tugging at the corner of his lips. "Works for those Silicon Valley CEOs."

"Oh, come on. You're just being lazy."

"I'm not!" he protested, but he was laughing as he said it.

"Pleeeeeeeease," she said, batting her eyelashes.

He laughed loudly. "Very…um, persuasive."

She poked his arm. "Stop laughing at me."

"Then stop making me laugh!"

"Come on. I saw lots of cute outfits at The Baby Boutique when I was there this morning to buy the wrap."

He sighed. "I have to admit…money's a little tight right now."

"No problem. They have a huge selection of secondhand baby clothes, and you can get them for, like, fifty cents a piece!"

"You really think anybody cares what he wears?" he asked, but he was opening his door as he said it.

"*I* care," she insisted, getting out.

He shook his head as he unclipped the baby from his car seat. "Five dollars, Blondie. That's all I can spare for more clothes."

She gave a brisk nod. "I can work with that."

She led the way to the boutique, a specialty store that was packed with an assortment of baby toys, furniture and clothes racks that were practically bursting with baby garments of all colors, shapes and sizes.

Rosalee Ward, the fiftysomething former fashion model who owned the store, was pinning a maternity shirt on the mama mannequin in the window. Dressed in a maxi skirt and an embroidered blouse, with her silver-blond hair up in a messy chignon, the woman looked effortlessly chic, as always, in a free-flowing, relaxed kind of way.

She looked up, pins in her mouth, when Chloe, Steve and Aiden walked in.

"Hi, hi, hi!" she said, the pins in her hand now, then pointed upward and grinned mischievously at the little sprig of mistletoe hanging over their heads. "Merry Christmas!"

"Oh, um…" Chloe looked from the mistletoe to Steve, feeling embarrassed.

To her surprise, his gaze was fixed on her lips. Her heart rate picked up. *What is going on here?* Did he still think about her in a romantic way?

Then he leaned down, the baby between them, and gave her a quick kiss on the cheek. "Merry Christmas," he murmured, close enough that she could smell the cedar and spice in his aftershave, and a little shot of awareness went through her, surprising her again.

Seriously, Chloe? It was your cheek. What in the world?

She peeked up to see if the same shock she was feeling was reflected on Steve's face, but he wasn't looking at her anymore, and his expression was stoic.

She felt the air leak out of her. Attraction wasn't just worthless—it was a traitor. She shouldn't be responding like this to the man who broke her teenage heart.

"Rosalee," Chloe said, working hard to make sure her voice didn't wobble or sound breathless. "Have you met Steve Weston? He just bought Family Physio, that physical therapy clinic down the street."

"Well, hello, Steve," Rosalee proclaimed cheerfully, her eyes not on Steve but on the baby. "And who's this handsome young fellow?"

"This is my nephew, Aiden," Steve said, sounding completely unaffected by that stupid kiss on the cheek. Just like that summer at church camp. After their kiss on the beach, she'd been the one who'd waited for weeks for him to call her. She'd been the one who'd been so smitten—and then so crushed—she could hardly concentrate on school.

So, if that kiss under the mistletoe hadn't affected him, she wasn't going to let it affect her, either.

"Oh, hello, young man! Hello!" Rosalee cooed at Aiden, nearly jabbing Chloe with the pins as she handed them over so she could grab the baby's feet and wiggle them around. "You are just precious, aren't you? Yes, you are!" She looked up at Steve, pushing a strand of silver hair out of her face. "Can I hold him?"

"Uh, sure," he said, handing Aiden over.

"Oh, what a sweet, sweet boy you are!" Rosalee cried, hugging the baby close. He squawked a little, but he didn't cry. Chloe knew that Rosalee was waiting—very impatiently—for her newly married daughter and son-in-law to make her a grandma.

"We're going to browse the secondhand section, okay, Rosalee?" Chloe said.

Not taking her eyes off Aiden, the older woman nodded and said, "Take all the time you need."

Chloe found the newborn racks and started whisking her way through the clothes, Steve standing awkwardly at her heels. She wanted to make him suffer a little for the feelings he'd evoked in her under the mistletoe, so she took her time examining the clothes before pulling out a little sailor suit. "This one's cute, isn't it?"

He shrugged. "Sure, looks nice."

She whipped out another outfit, this one with little baby chicks all over it. "How about this one?"

"Yeah, all right."

"Or this one?" She held up some pajamas with a pattern of yellow-and-green guitars.

"Whatever you want, Blondie."

She arched an eyebrow. "You have no opinion whatsoever?"

He shrugged again, but it looked as though he was trying to tamp down a smile. "I'd be fine dressing him in the same outfit every day."

"So, I can pick *anything* I want?"

"As long as you don't buy a bunch of holiday costumes, sure."

Laughing, she pulled a onesie from the rack. "How about this one?" It said, *If I look funny, it's because Daddy dressed me.*

He put his hands on his hips. "Ha, ha."

"Okay, fine. We won't get that one. How about—" She pulled a black-and-white-striped, long-sleeved onesie that read *Just did 9 months on the inside* off the rack with a flourish. "This one?"

Instead of laughing, as she'd anticipated, Steve went pale. "No," he said flatly. "Put that one back."

"Oh," she replied, taken aback by his tone. "What's wrong?"

"It's fine," he said, but his voice was tight.

She looked at the offending piece of clothing as though it could explain his strange reaction. Yes, she'd been giving him a hard time, but all in the name of fun. She hadn't wanted to actually upset him. "I was just kidding around."

"I know," he said, and his tone was gentler now. "And it's fine. But here—" He took his wallet out of his back pocket and handed her a five-dollar bill. "Why don't you finish up on your own? I should get Aiden back home."

"Oh, okay."

He must have heard the confusion in her voice because he sighed and said, "My dad's in prison, Blondie. Has been for a long time."

Her breath hitched and her eyes went round. She had *not* been expecting that at all. "I'm sorry," she said. "I didn't know."

"It's fine. We should go, that's all. You can get home on your own, can't you?"

She gave a little laugh, but it was devoid of humor. "It's one block away, Weston. I can manage."

He nodded and held out the money to her again. "Okay, we'll get out of your hair. Leave the shopping to the expert."

After he and Aiden walked out, she turned her attention back to the clothes racks, feeling awful. He hadn't said much to her about his parents back when they were teenagers, and she wondered if his dad's criminal history was part of the reason why.

She wondered how long his dad had been incarcerated, and whether he'd been in prison when Steve was growing up. Either way, it had to be hard to deal with emotionally.

And now he had to cope with his sister's death on top of that, too.

And care for a newborn baby.

A swell of sympathy rose up inside her, displacing the lingering resentment she felt over his disappearance eleven years ago. Regardless of what had happened between them back then, Steve was going through a lot, and she'd do her best to let go of the past and be there to support him now.

Aunt Mabel leaned heavily on Steve's arm as they walked up the aisle of Wychmere Community Church on Sunday morning. He was quite concerned about her lack of mobility these days.

He'd tried to convince her to bring her cane to church this morning, but she'd steadfastly refused. "I've been going to church on my own for years now, Steven. I know how to take care of myself."

Although he'd been faithful about calling her twice a week ever since he'd gone away to the

University of Rhode Island, he'd only seen her a handful of times since his granddad's funeral, and her physical condition had deteriorated a good deal since then. Before Eloise had died, they'd both tried to talk to her about selling her house and moving into an assisted living facility, but she'd shot that idea down almost before it was out of their mouths.

She'd fought them tooth and nail on getting a medical alert device, too, but Steve and Eloise had prevailed on that one in the end. And good thing, too. Aunt Mabel's arthritis had gotten so bad that she was now having trouble walking and doing such simple things as pouring a glass of water, turning a faucet and opening the door.

"I'd really feel better about it if you'd bring your cane to church."

Aunt Mabel patted his cheek. "Just lend me your arm, dear. All will be well."

They reached what his great-aunt told him was her customary seat: third row from the front, off to the left, next to Irene Perkins, Chloe's seventysomething roommate and owner of the local candy shop, and a few other of the town's elderly widows.

Aside from Eloise's funeral, he hadn't been to church in years. Not because he didn't believe, but because—after what his father had done—he'd felt so ashamed, and so judged.

The people in his hometown certainly hadn't been shy about transferring their contempt of his father onto him. He'd heard all the whispers in the hallways at school, felt the stares of the little old ladies and the righteous old men at church.

And although he'd done his best to prove that he would never, ever, do the kinds of things his father had done, it hadn't been until he'd left New Hampshire to go to university that he'd felt any relief from the shattering weight of other people's lack of belief in him.

He'd never wanted to feel that way again, and so—even though he knew it was irrational— he'd avoided church for fear that the people there would see right through him. See inside him. Know what kind of weak stock he came from and turn him away.

But being here, now, with so many other believers, felt comforting, like coming home to a mug of warm apple cider after snowshoeing on a cold winter day.

Steve had a good view of the altar, decorated simply with poinsettias and a silver star, and a good view of the choir. A good view of Chloe, too, seated at the piano in a green Christmas sweater. It was too early yet for the entrance hymn, but she was playing something soft and soothing as people filtered into the little white clapboard church.

He was angry with himself for the way he'd reacted to her picking up that silly onesie at the clothing store yesterday, and worried that he'd scared her off from working as Aiden's nanny. But seeing her took the edge off his anxiety. The restful music helped, too.

He'd hurt her feelings. Those big brown eyes of hers had first gone very round and then they'd filled with confusion at his abrupt reaction to that ridiculous outfit.

He wished he could take it back, his kneejerk response to seeing that thing. It was a harmless little baby suit, nothing more.

But he was touchy about things like that, he wouldn't deny it. For almost as long as he could remember, he'd wished for a different father—a father like his friend Liam's, who'd practically adopted Steve, taking him to Boy Scout meetings and baseball practices and Sunday services with his own family when Steve's father had been nowhere to be found.

Steve was incredibly grateful for Liam and his family. Without them, without the faith they'd helped him find so young, he honestly didn't know where he'd be right now.

Dead, like his mother?

In prison, like his dad?

Steve wanted no part of his father's legacy,

but when he looked in the mirror, there was no denying that he was his father's son.

That wasn't Chloe's fault, though, and he hoped the way he'd walked out on her at the clothing store wouldn't make her rethink accepting the job as Aiden's nanny. He needed her. Because of the money he owed, he needed her a lot.

The congregation stood and sang "O Little Town of Bethlehem." There were announcements, greetings and prayers. Then the pastor, a fairly young guy in casual clothes and glasses, asked everyone to open their Bibles and read Luke 17:3–4, which was all about forgiveness.

Steve squirmed uncomfortably in his seat, thinking about the letters his father had written to Eloise, the ones Steve had only seen after she'd died.

The ones he'd been convinced his father had only written so Eloise would write a letter on his behalf to the parole board.

But what if he was wrong?

After skimming a few of the letters, Steve had thrown them in the trash. His father had sent *him* letters earlier in his sentence. Steve had marked them "Return to Sender" and put them straight back in the mail. He'd never wanted to hear his father's excuses.

But what if they weren't just excuses? What if his father was legitimately attempting to make amends?

He curled his fist in his lap. *He can't make amends for what he did*, Steve reminded himself fiercely. *She's dead. She's gone.*

Pastor Nate looked out at the congregation. He took off his glasses and pinched the bridge of his nose. "It's a tall order, isn't it? To be hurt again and again and still forgive?"

The pastor surveyed the people sitting in front of him. "As we prepare our hearts to celebrate the birth of Our Lord and Savior, remember that hurt people hurt other people. And we're all hurt. We're all broken. But with God's help, every single one of us can change."

He then asked everyone to read the next couple of verses, but Aiden got fussy, and Steve had to take him outside. He walked around the front of the church, admiring the life-sized nativity scene set up on the lawn, until Aiden fell asleep in the baby wrap.

The air was crisp and the ground was crunchy now that the grass had dried out in preparation for the next frost. Steve drew the sides of his jacket tight over Aiden's sleeping form, protecting him from the chill.

Was the pastor right? Could *anyone* change?

Or was even entertaining the thought that his father might have been sincere in his letters the biggest joke of all time?

Just as Steve was about to head back into the church, people started coming out. After a few minutes, Aunt Mabel and her friend Irene appeared, escorted by his old friend, Brett.

"There you are!" Aunt Mabel exclaimed, slowly making her way in his direction, leaning heavily—and shakily—on Brett's arm.

Brett, who'd always been bigger than him, gave him a big grin and held out his hand as he approached. "Steve Weston! Long time no see, brother."

Steve shook his hand. "How's it going, Brett?"

Brett's grin practically split his face. "Well, I've got two lovely ladies on my arm, so it's going pretty good."

Aunt Mabel giggled.

"I had to fight off the older guys with a stick to get to them, though. That Bill Anderson," Brett said, winking at Irene, "he's a persistent guy."

Irene swatted him on the arm. "Oh, stop."

Brett smiled and gestured toward Steve's jacket. "Heard there's a pretty cute baby you've been hiding from us."

Steve peeled back the side of his coat to show

Brett the baby. Aiden was still asleep. "Here he is."

"Sweet, brother. Gotta get me one of those."

Steve laughed. "You're married?" He hadn't kept in touch with any of his friends from Cape Cod after he left all those years ago, but he was happy that he and Brett seemed to be picking up right where they'd left off.

Brett shook his head. "Gotta get me a wife, too."

Aunt Mabel chucked Brett's cheek. "You boys. Any girl would be blessed to have you."

Brett smirked at Steve. "Well, if the lovely Ms. *Mabel* says so, it *must* be true…"

Irene, who seemed to be quite the spitfire for a senior citizen, rolled her eyes. "It *is* true, Bartholomew. You've been gun-shy ever since that girl in Boston turned down your proposal, but you can't let that stop you. You need to grab happiness by the reins and get back on the horse."

"Bartholomew?" Steve repeated, trying not to laugh.

Brett gave him a dark look. "It's a family name, my man. My dad let my mom put it on my birth certificate, but he insisted on calling me Brett, so don't go getting any ideas." Then he directed Irene to latch onto Steve's arm. "Help me escort these lovely ladies to the hall for some donuts, would you? Then we can catch up."

Steve obliged. They brought Irene and Mabel to the church hall, then got them situated at a card table with some of their friends.

"So, what you been up to, Weston? I heard about your sister. That's rough, man. I'm sorry."

Steve nodded. "Thanks."

"And you roped *my* sister into taking care of the baby, huh?"

"Uh, I wouldn't say I roped her into anything…"

Brett smirked. "I'm just messing with you. She's happy to have the job. Even if you *did* break her heart way back when."

Steve froze. He broke her heart?

Brett started laughing. "I'm messing with you again, Weston. That was a long time ago. She's over it."

Steve gave an uneasy chuckle. Should he try to explain himself? He never told people what had happened back in New Hampshire that night. But maybe it was time to let down his defenses, and Brett had once been a good friend…

"Mr. Bwett! Mr. Bwett!" A cute little girl with long brown hair and big green eyes ran up to Brett and launched herself at his legs. Her dress was pink and sparkly, and the soles of her shoes lit up when she ran.

"Hey, sweetheart," Brett said, scooping her up into his arms. "Say hello to Mr. Steve."

The girl pushed a strand of hair out of her face. "Hi, Mr. Steve."

Brett hoisted the girl higher. "Steve, Emma. Emma, Steve."

"Hi, Emma," Steve said.

She jutted her little chin at his jacket, which was still covering Aiden. She *definitely* had donut crumbs on her face. "Why are you so lumpy?"

He grinned. "Can you keep a secret?"

She nodded solemnly.

He slid the zipper on his jacket down a tiny bit, just enough to show her the top of Aiden's head. "I'm hiding a baby in here."

Her eyes went very big. Her voice got very breathless. "A baby!" She looked up at Brett. "Put me down! Put me down!"

He set her on the floor and she ran to a nearby table, then practically dragged a man in a suit and a woman in a green dress over to Steve and Brett. "Mommy! Mr. Jonafin! Look! A baby!"

The man laughed and ruffled her hair. Then he held out his hand to Steve. "Jonathan Masters."

Steve shook his hand. "Steve Weston."

"This is my fiancée, Laura," Jonathan said, putting a possessive arm around the pretty brunette who was clearly the little girl's mom.

The woman smiled up at Steve, her eyes twinkling. "We've met."

"Have we?" She looked vaguely familiar to him, but he couldn't place her.

"Church camp, here at WCC? A long time ago."

That's when it clicked. "You're Chloe's friend, right?"

She smiled bigger. "Guilty as charged."

"Nice to see you again."

"We're headed back to the church sanctuary for pageant practice." She glanced between Brett and Steve. "Do you two want to join us? Chloe's up there, helping the kids learn the Christmas carols."

Brett quirked his head to the side and looked to Steve, who went over to check with his great-aunt.

"Of course, dear," she said, shooing him back to his friends. "It'll be good for you to have some fun."

They all trekked to the church, where roughly twenty kids ranging from age three to thirteen were gathered around Chloe at the altar. Emma ran up to the front, while Laura, Jonathan, Steve and Brett sat in a pew near the back.

"Emma's playing the Star of Bethlehem in the pageant," Laura told Steve, leaning over Jonathan, who had his arm around her shoulders again. "She's beyond excited for her five minutes of fame."

"Cute. Does she have to memorize lines?"

Laura shook her head. "None of the kids do, except for the angel Gabriel. But they've got an older kid playing that role, so he'll be fine. The little ones just walk onto the altar in their costumes while the narrator reads the Christmas story from the Bible, pausing whenever there's a relevant hymn."

"It's an annual tradition," Brett chimed in. "Everyone comes to the Christmas Eve pageant. And then there's a big potluck supper afterward."

"It used to be in the church hall," Laura said, her eyes lighting up, "but we're having it at The Sea Glass Inn this year. Two o'clock, right after the pageant. You should come!"

Aiden smacked his lips and squirmed, and Steve adjusted him in the wrap. "I'm not much of a cook. I don't know what I could contribute."

Brett gave a loud guffaw and punched him on the arm. "Don't be ridiculous, Weston. Nobody expects you to bring anything when you've got a new baby."

Laura put her hands together in a beseeching gesture. "In addition to the food, we'll have games and caroling. You have to come!"

Jonathan smiled at him. "You can always pick

up some dinner rolls at the store if you don't want to show up empty-handed."

"I'll check with Aunt Mabel, but it does sound like fun," Steve said. In fact, it sounded much better than what he'd done on Christmas Eve last year: a full shift at his old physical therapy practice in Providence, followed by a take-out turkey dinner from Denny's, which he'd eaten in front of the TV after trying—and failing—to get in touch with Eloise.

Laura chuckled. "Mabel's already RSVP'd. She and Irene have been looking forward to this for months."

"In that case," Steve said, "how can I say no?"

They sat and watched the rehearsal for a few minutes, and then Aiden started to cry. Steve excused himself to make Aiden a bottle. Brett followed along, watching with interest as Steve took out the water and formula and then mixed it up. "You're good at this," Brett said, nodding at the bottle.

Steve snorted. "Practice makes perfect, I guess. This whole thing has been an exercise in getting thrown in the deep end."

"You want to have your own kids one day?"

Steve hitched his shoulder, careful not to jostle Aiden, who was happily drinking his bottle. "Never saw myself as a family man." In reality, he didn't want to pass down his father's DNA. Holding his nephew, though, made him wonder about that decision.

Brett ran a hand through his dark hair. "I have. I love kids. They're the best."

"No romantic prospects at the moment, though?" Steve asked, remembering Irene's comment about Brett's failed proposal.

Brett sighed. "No. I almost signed up for one of those dating apps, but after what happened to Chloe…"

Steve went still. "What happened to Chloe?"

"I don't wanna gossip, but she met some creep who was seeing other women at the same time."

Steve scowled. What man would want to date other women when he could date Chloe?

"Don't tell her I said anything, though. She'll be mad." Brett paused for a second. "So, what about you, Weston? You got someone special?"

Steve shook his head. "I don't date much." *At all* is what he'd have said if he were being honest. But he didn't get honest about it with anyone. He knew they'd try to reason with him, use logic to talk him into doing something he didn't want to do: inflict his sorry DNA on some unsuspecting woman.

Brett grinned. "We can remedy that, brother. Lots of ladies sit up and take notice when a new man moves to town."

Steve nodded to where Aiden was cradled in his arms. "Uh, I don't really have time for that right now…"

Brett smirked. "Women dig babies, Weston."

Steve laughed. "I'll take that under advisement."

"You been to Franco's since you been back?" Brett asked, referring to the pizza parlor on Main Street the two of them had frequented as teens.

"Not yet."

"Wanna go for lunch?"

"Um…" Steve nodded to the baby again.

"We'll see if we can convince Chloe, Laura and Jonathan to come along. I bet we can talk the girls into holding the baby."

"Mind if I drop my aunt off at home first?" Steve asked, starting to feel excited about the idea. It had been a long time since he'd had the chance to spend an afternoon with friends.

"Take your time. We'll meet you there."

Steve situated Aiden in the wrap and went to get Aunt Mabel. He was looking forward to spending more time with Brett, but most of all, he was hoping to see Chloe.

Having lunch with her at the pizza parlor would give him a chance to smooth things over from yesterday. He wanted to make sure she'd stay on as Aiden's nanny, but he also couldn't stand the thought that she might be upset with him.

If what Brett had said about him breaking her heart was true, he'd hurt her enough when they were teenagers. He didn't want to do it again now.

Chapter Five

Chloe placed the sheet music from the Christmas carols for the pageant back on the shelf in the music room. Ever since she'd seen Steve sitting at the back of the church with her brother and her friends, she'd felt jittery, which annoyed her. He wasn't her teenage crush anymore—he was her boss!

But maybe her jitters weren't about the spark of attraction she'd felt yesterday under the mistletoe; maybe they were about the fact that his father was in prison and she'd unwittingly called attention to that fact.

She'd spent all night wondering *why* Steve's father was in jail, but just as she wasn't going to ask him why he'd disappeared all those summers ago, she wasn't going to ask him about his dad's criminal history, either. If he wanted to tell her, fine. If he didn't, it wasn't her business, anyway.

She worked for him—he wasn't her crush, and they weren't friends.

Laura opened the door and poked her head into the music room. "There you are!" she exclaimed. She was wearing an emerald-colored wrap dress that Chloe had helped her pick out, and it made her green eyes pop. "We're heading to Franco's for lunch. You want to come along?"

Chloe slid the last of the sheet music into place. "Sure."

"Awesome." Laura grinned. "Steve's joining us, too."

Chloe's heart skipped and she did her best to ignore it. *Not your crush, remember?* "I saw him sitting with you guys."

"Emma's in love with that baby."

Chloe chuckled. "Join the club."

"I invited them to the Christmas Eve potluck."

"Good," Chloe said. "I don't think Steve's had a chance to meet many people around town yet."

"We got a couple of reservations at the inn, too, so it's going to be a full house."

Laura had recently taken over as the property manager of The Sea Glass Inn, which her grandmother used to own. Previously, it had only been open during the summer tourist season, but this year, they were taking bookings over Christmas and New Year's.

Chloe gave Laura a little hug. "That's great! I know you were hoping it would take off."

Laura looked down, blushing happily. "Just two reservations so far, but there's a family with a little girl who's right around Emma's age, so that'll be awesome, plus a newly married couple with a baby on the way."

"Perfect for Christmastime," Chloe said, sighing. She was excited for her student teaching placement, but she couldn't deny that her biological clock was ticking, too. Before Dan's duplicity had come to light, it had seemed like he and Chloe were on the same page about what they wanted out of life. Love. Marriage. A family.

She still wanted those things, although she'd learned the hard way that she had to put herself first. Get her ducks in a row, get her career in order, then worry about finding a man she could have a family with someday.

That way, if things didn't work out, she wouldn't be stuck relying on Brett to bail her out.

"So." Laura winked at Chloe, who knew what was coming. This had been a running topic of conversation for them for the last six months. "Did you see the way Bill Anderson was looking at Irene?"

"I know! It's adorable. And she just ignores him. It's so sad."

"You should invite Bill over for dinner one night and then conveniently come up with a reason to leave the apartment right before you all sit down to eat."

Chloe chuckled. "Irene would not be happy."

"It's for her own good! Do you honestly think she's that clueless, or is it willful ignorance on her part?"

"She claims he's too young for her."

Laura shook her head in exasperation. "That's silly."

"I know."

"What's the age difference? Five years? Six?"

"Seven."

"That's nothing," Laura said, waving it off. "Same as me and Jonathan."

Chloe shrugged. "It's different when the woman's older."

"It shouldn't be."

"Anyway," Chloe said, heading for the door. "I hope someone looks at *me* like that one day."

Laura gave her a secretive smile. "One day might be closer than you think."

Chloe stopped to shoot her friend an inquisitive look. "What's that supposed to mean?"

"Steve had a hard time taking his eyes off you during the pageant practice."

Chloe snorted. "Only because I was front and center, leading the kids."

"Nope, I guarantee you, Jonathan and Brett weren't looking at you the way he was."

Chloe felt a little kick of excitement, but immediately pushed it down. She'd felt the same way yesterday under the mistletoe, while Steve had been completely unfazed.

She shook her head. "You're wrong. He might've been looking at me, but only to think about how insensitive I am."

She went on to tell Laura about their trip to The Baby Boutique and her faux pas with the onesie.

"Wow, poor Steve," Laura said. "That's a lot for one person to deal with."

"It almost makes me wish I wasn't about to leave for Boston so I could stay and help."

Laura gave her a worried look. "You're not going to put off your student teaching placement again, are you, Chlo?"

"I said *almost*, Laura. Almost."

"Good. You've worked too hard not to see it through this time."

"Trust me. I'm getting my degree if it's the last thing I do."

She'd do her best to support Steve now, while she was working for him. After Christmas, he was on his own.

* * *

Franco's Pizza Parlor was just like Steve remembered: a huge neon sign advertising Hot Pizza in the front window, and no-frills gray flooring and well-loved wooden tables and chairs inside. Over the big front counter was a chalkboard menu that listed all the items on offer: pizza, pasta, calzones, grinders, salads, garlic bread, chicken wings, French fries, meatballs and onion rings. There were a handful of arcade games in the corner, too.

The store had the warm, yeasty scent of baking bread with an overlay of garlicky tomato sauce. Franco himself, who stood behind the counter in a white apron and a red Santa hat, had a booming voice and a thunderous laugh.

Brett, Chloe, Laura, Jonathan and Emma were crowded around a couple of tables they'd pushed together. There were a few pizzas, a platter of wings and a large basket of fries in front of them.

"Weston," Brett called out when Steve entered, waving him over. "Help us get rid of this food."

He sat in the open seat next to Chloe, and his heart lifted the same way it had back when they were teens. From the moment he'd first seen her, he'd always loved being around her. Clearly, that hadn't changed in the intervening years.

She smiled and reached for Aiden. "Glad you could join us."

"How'd the shopping expedition turn out?" he asked, broaching the subject of how he'd acted at the clothing store yesterday. Would she forgive him for freaking out like that? Or would she hold a grudge?

"It was fine," she said carefully.

"You find some good clothes?"

"I found a couple things."

"I'm sorry I snapped at you."

"It was my fault," she said, moving Aiden from the crook of her arm to her shoulder. "If I'd known, I never would have—"

He touched her elbow. "You couldn't have known. I don't talk about it with anyone."

Her eyes, when she looked at him, were dark as molasses, and his breath caught in his throat. He'd always thought she was beautiful. And her eyes. A man could drown in them if he wasn't careful.

Needing to lighten the mood, he reached past her to snag a French fry and said, "You proved me right this morning, you know."

Her eyebrows shot up.

"Definitely a rock star vibe."

She laughed. "Yeah, I'm sure all the big rock bands are dying to get me and my piano rendition of 'Go Tell It on the Mountain' on their next world tour."

"Seriously, though. You're talented."

She snorted.

"You are," he insisted. "And great with the kids."

She blushed. "You don't have to butter me up, Weston. I'm not mad at you."

He opened his mouth to protest, but Brett, from his end of the table, commanded, "Enough with the chitchat, sis. Let the man eat."

Chloe's cheeks pinked. "For your information, *Bartholomew*," she announced, leveling her brother with a stare, "*he* was talking to *me*."

Brett smirked. "Yeah, right."

Chloe's cheeks went outright red, but before she could reply, Steve jumped in. "She's right, dude. I've got eleven years of town gossip to catch up on."

Brett gave him a suspicious look, but Steve just stared back at him, sporting a bland smile. He remembered the way Chloe and Brett squabbled, siblings who were only one year apart.

Brett shoved a paper plate at him. "Whatever, man. The more talking, the less time we have to play," he said, jerking his head in the direction of the arcade games.

"Aunt Chloe," Emma piped up, "can I hold the baby?"

Chloe shot a quick, questioning look at Steve while Laura said, "Emma, honey, you need to ask Mr. Steve, not Aunt Chloe."

"Mr. Steve," Emma said solemnly, "can I pwease, pwease, pwease hold the baby? I pwomise I won't dwop him."

"Do you want to hold him together with your aunt Chloe?" he asked.

"Okay," she said.

"Then sure."

"Yay!" Emma cried.

Laura stood and helped Emma get situated on Chloe's lap. Steve ate his pizza, amused at how even the smallest of the female species seemed drawn to infants. Maybe Brett was right. Girls *did* like babies.

Before too long, Brett and Jonathan ushered Steve away from the table and up to the arcade games. He was rusty at pinball but still pretty good at Pac-Man. Brett and Jonathan definitely had some kind of ongoing competition, and they were both good at all the games. The best pinball player by far, though, was Laura, who clinched the machine's second-highest score of all time.

She threw her hands in the air in victory. "Beat that, boys!"

Jonathan grinned and looked at Emma. "What do you say, Tiny? Should we take Mommy out for an ice cream cone to celebrate?"

"Ice cweam, ice cweam, you're so good! We eat you way more than we should!" Emma shouted at the top of her lungs.

Laura and Jonathan both laughed. "Anyone else care to join us?" Jonathan said, standing.

Steve shook his head. "I should get Aiden home."

"I need to get going, too," Chloe added.

"I'll join you," Brett said. "I've always got room for ice cream."

They cleared their table and put on their jackets, then headed to the door en masse. Steve quietly tried to offer Brett and Jonathan some money for lunch, but they waved it away, and he was secretly relieved.

Outside, Laura, Jonathan, Emma and Brett headed to the left for their trek to the ice cream parlor.

Steve turned to Chloe. "Did you drive?"

She shook her head. "Candy Shack's just two blocks away."

"Can I walk you?"

"It's really not far."

He shrugged. "It'll be nice to get some fresh air."

She started walking and he followed, Aiden safely secured in the sling. "How'd that happen, anyway? You living with Irene at The Candy Shack?"

She smirked. "Well, it's probably not hard to see that Brett still drives me up the wall."

He smothered a smile. Nope, it wasn't hard to see at all.

"After he moved back home, the house felt way too small. Irene's husband had just passed away, and she was lonely, so she offered to let me move in. It's been good for us both. To not be alone."

"Your parents weren't able to referee for you and Brett?"

Chloe's breath hitched and she stopped walking. "My parents died, Weston. A few years ago now. Car wreck."

His heart fell. He'd spent a lot of time at the Richardson house playing video games with Brett the summer he was seventeen, and her parents had been good people. "Aw, Blondie. I'm sorry."

She gave him a half smile, but her eyes were sad. "You know how it goes."

He did, but that didn't make it easier. "I lost my mom a while back, too."

"It's tough sometimes, isn't it?" she said rhetorically, giving his arm a squeeze before starting to walk again.

They continued on in silence for a moment, and then he blurted out, "You're going to keep working for me, aren't you?"

She looked taken aback by his question. "What? Why wouldn't I?"

He gave Aiden's head a little pat. "I thought maybe I scared you off yesterday, at the clothing store."

She laughed. "You worry too much, Weston. I already told you I'm not mad at you. And anyway, it would take a lot more than that to scare me off. I've wanted to be a teacher for a long time, and I just kept putting it off and putting it off because other people needed me here. My parents, with the restaurant. Then Brett, also with the restaurant. And then Dan, with…" She waved her hand dismissively. "Well, that doesn't matter. But I'm *this close* to finally making that dream a reality. Believe me when I tell you that, as long as you pay me, I can handle anything you throw at me. Because I'm going to Boston in January to finish my teaching degree, and this time *nothing's* going to stand in my way."

They stopped in front of The Candy Shack, with its red vinyl siding and its covered porch and its flower boxes in the windows upstairs. Chloe was breathing hard, her face impassioned.

What would it be like if she had the same kind of feelings for you?

Aiden let out a little cry and Steve patted his back through the sling, pushing the thought out of his head. He had nothing to offer her. She wasn't angry with him and she was going to keep working for him. That would have to be enough.

"I'm glad you're pursuing your dream, Blondie. You deserve to be happy." He didn't know what else to say.

She gave him an odd look—maybe that had been the wrong thing to say?—then leaned in to pat Aiden on the head. "See you tomorrow, then?"

Steve nodded. "See you tomorrow."

He tried not to feel disappointed when she walked away.

Chapter Six

Over the next week, Chloe and Steve settled into a routine. She'd arrive at Steve's house at 8:30 a.m. and chat with him for a few minutes before he left for work, taking her car so she'd have access to his car and the baby's car seat while he was gone.

After that, she'd take Aiden for a walk, give him a bath or play with him on his play mat for a while before he took a bottle and had his first nap. When he was sleeping, she had the chance to straighten up Steve's house, and even do some of her online coursework.

In the afternoons, as Steve had requested, she'd take Aiden over to Mabel's cottage. Steve was worried that his great-aunt was having trouble getting around and doing basic household chores, and he'd asked Chloe to take care of them for her under the guise of letting Mabel play with the baby.

Mabel adored Aiden and was immensely thankful that Chloe was willing to bring him by, often lamenting the fact that her arthritis prevented her from being able to hold him. So, while Aiden kicked in his bouncy chair or lay on his play mat, Chloe would do Mabel's dishes and water her plants.

On Friday afternoon, Chloe took Aiden to The Sea Glass Inn after they visited with Mabel so she could help Laura wrap some gifts for the giving tree at church. She was running a little late, so she was surprised when she got back to Steve's place and saw he wasn't home.

He called a couple minutes later, sounding stressed. "Aunt Mabel fell. We're at the hospital right now. They need to do some blood tests and X-rays. I know you're supposed to be on your way home already, but I don't want to leave her here all by herself until they know what's going on. Is there any chance you could stay longer to watch the baby?"

"Oh, my gosh, of course. Stay as late as you need to. Is Mabel okay?"

He let out an audible breath. "She's in pain, but they just gave her something for it, so hopefully she'll be a little more comfortable now. They're worried she broke her hip."

"Oh, no!"

"Yeah, they're talking about surgery."

"Poor Mabel!"

"Hang on a second." He must have put his hand over the speaker because she heard muffled voices in the background before he came back on the line. "Sorry. That was the nurse."

"Steve, can I do anything for you? Call anybody? Bring dinner?"

"We're still in the ER. I think it's best if we just wait and see what happens."

"Do you have any other family you need me to call?"

"No." He sighed. "Just me."

"Okay, well, don't worry about us. Aiden's good, and I can stay as long as you need, all right? Hang in there and let Mabel know I'm praying for her."

He sighed again. "Thanks, Blondie. I don't know what I'd do without you."

They hung up, leaving her feeling at loose ends. She prayed, she paced with Aiden, she put him down and stretched her sore back. She was grateful for this job, but carting the baby around so much wasn't doing her herniated disks any favors.

When Aiden went down for a short nap, she made a big pot of pasta—stretching her culinary skills about as far as they could go. Unlike Brett, who'd inherited his love of cooking from their parents, Chloe had never been a big fan of the kitchen. Her lack of interest in the culinary arts had actually caused a lot of friction between her and her mother.

Although Chloe had stayed in town to help her parents run the restaurant after Brett had joined the navy, she hadn't been very gracious about it. It probably would have been better for her relationship with her mom if she'd just followed her heart in the first place and pursued her teaching degree right after high school.

Apparently she was a slow learner, though, because when Brett came back to Wychmere Bay after they died and begged her to stay on as the general manager of Half Shell, at least until he got his bearings, she'd acquiesced—against her better judgment once again.

And when Dan had asked her, just this past summer, to put off her student teaching placement so they could see where their relationship was heading, she'd given in *again*.

All for a man who'd married someone else without a backward glance!

Honestly, how many times did she have to make the same mistake before it would sink in? Allowing other people to dictate the course of her life would never make her happy. She was the captain of her own ship, the master of her own destiny. If she didn't stand up for what she wanted, no one else would do it for her.

Which was why she was determined to make this student teaching job in Boston work. Boston hadn't been her first choice, but she wasn't going to let anything stand in the way of her achieving her dream ever again.

Not the high cost of city living.

Not the fact that it was so far from her big galoot of a brother, who was both intensely annoying and fiercely lovable.

Not the fact that she'd be leaving all her friends.

Nope, none of that was going to stop her this time. This time, she was sailing straight to Teacher Town.

Shaking her head at the ridiculousness of that phrase, Chloe waited for the water to boil, then poured a package of spaghetti into the pot. Since making spaghetti required little more than boiling water and giving the noodles an occasional stir, she was able to navigate it okay, even with her subpar cooking skills. And it would be easy enough for Steve to reheat in the microwave, so it was a win-win.

Aiden woke up and she gave him another bottle. When he was done, Chloe clipped him into his bouncy chair, where he waved his arms, all herky-jerky, at the little plastic toys hanging from the bar overhead. Then she portioned out the now-clumpy spaghetti into bowls, poured some pasta sauce and frozen meatballs on top and covered them with plastic wrap.

Mission accomplished. It might not be gourmet, but at least Steve would have some grab-and-go meals at the ready for the weekend.

She felt bad for the guy. Once she'd gotten over her teenage heartache and emerged from the fog of her depression, she'd spent a lot of time fuming about how he'd hidden his true character from her. Now she wasn't so sure that was the case.

He didn't seem like a jerk. He seemed like someone who was trying his best to navigate some difficult circumstances. His sister's death. His new business opening. His nephew—and now his great-aunt—needing care.

And if he *had* been a jerk as a teenager? Well, as she'd said to Laura, that was a long time ago.

At seven o'clock, she started Aiden's bedtime routine. Bath, fresh pajamas, bottle. There was a rocking chair in his nursery, and she sat there to feed him. It would have been nice if Steve had bought a Christmas tree for the family room, because then she could have enjoyed looking at the tree while Aiden had his nighttime feed, but she doubted he'd have a chance to get one now that Mabel was in the hospital.

Aiden fell asleep when he got to the last ounce, and she eased the bottle out of his mouth, careful not to jostle him awake. She sat with him in the dark until he stopped twitching, then she laid him in his crib and tiptoed from the room.

When she came out, Steve was sitting at the kitchen table, staring at his hands.

"Hey," she whispered, sliding into the chair across from him. "How's Mabel?"

He looked up, his face drawn. "It's a fracture. They're going to do surgery on Monday."

She sucked in a breath. "I'm sorry, Steve. How awful."

He ran a hand through his hair, then dragged it down the side of his face. "I hate to ask, but can you help me with Aiden over the weekend? I don't want to leave her in the hospital all alone."

"Of course you don't," she said. "Don't give it another thought. I'm happy to help."

"I don't, um…" He looked down. "I don't think I can pay you for it. The weekend, I mean."

She honestly hadn't been thinking about the money. After all, what kind of Scrooge would she have to be to leave Mabel to suffer by herself in the hospital right before Christmas? "It's all right, Weston. We'll figure something out."

"See, that's the thing, Blondie. I'm not sure we will figure it out." His expression was tense, almost pained.

"What do you mean?"

"My sister's funeral put me thousands of dollars in debt. I think I'm going to lose my clinic."

Chloe's expression didn't change, and Steve started to panic. If she walked out as Aiden's nanny, he was doomed.

"I spent most of my savings on the down payment for the clinic, and then when Eloise died, I had to put her funeral expenses on my credit card. I had to cancel almost two weeks' worth of appointments, too, so there was no income coming in to help cover my costs. And I'll have to cancel more appointments to stay at the hospital with Aunt Mabel for the surgery."

He scrubbed at his face again. Anxiety crackled inside him like an electrical wire writhing on the ground. He was talking too much, but he couldn't stop himself. It all just came spilling out. "I have a couple of months before I'll default on the business loan, but at the rate I'm going, I can't see how I'm going to keep things afloat."

Chloe just stared at him. This was going even worse than he'd thought.

"I'm sorry. I didn't mean to dump all that on you."

She studied him a moment longer. "Have you eaten?"

He blinked. "What?"

"Dinner? Have you eaten dinner?"

He took a quick look at his watch. It was after eight o'clock. He hadn't been aware of it before, but now that she'd mentioned it, he found that he *was* hungry. "No."

She got up. "I made spaghetti."

"Uh…thanks?"

"I'll pop it in the microwave for you."

"You don't have to—"

"It's fine. Sit. Let me help."

He watched her flit around his kitchen, pulling a bowl out of the refrigerator and two cups out of a cupboard.

"Water?" she asked.

He nodded. "Sure."

She filled the two cups and brought them to the table. He took one and sipped while she went and retrieved his bowl of pasta from the microwave. She set it down in front of him. "Here. It might be hot."

He looked at the bowl in front of him. He looked at her. Was this her way of softening the blow when she let him know she wouldn't be working for him anymore?

He closed his eyes to say a quick blessing. Whatever else was about to happen, the pasta sauce smelled good.

"I know your mom died, and your dad's in prison," she said, watching him from across the table, her eyes dark and unreadable, "but do you have any other family? Anybody who might be able to help you out?"

He shook his head. "My mom was an only child, and Aunt Mabel never had any children. My dad's side of the family... He had a couple of brothers, but I never really knew them. After Mom died, we didn't stay in touch."

"Do you think you could track them down?"

He gave his head a hard shake. "They're not good people, Blondie. I wouldn't want to find them even if I could."

He was relieved when she didn't try to argue with him, just dipped her head in acknowledgment. "Have you talked to anyone about this besides me? Pastor Nate, maybe? Or Brett?"

He stared into his bowl of pasta, his appetite waning. The shame of not being able to support himself financially was almost as bad as the shame of being his father's son. "No."

"Can I talk to them about it?" she asked.

"I'd really rather you didn't."

She sighed. "You're part of this community now, Steve. People are going to want to support you."

"I hardly know anyone here."

"You know me and Brett. And everybody knows Mabel."

"I'm not someone who asks for charity."

She tilted her head to the side as though trying to figure him out, her blond hair framing her face, which was luminous in the light from the lamp overhead. She didn't say anything, but her eyes were so expressive he could practically read her mind. *You don't ask for charity from anyone except me.*

He hung his head. "I'm sorry." He shouldn't have asked. He shouldn't have told her what he'd told her. He was going to lose the clinic anyway—at least by keeping his mouth shut he'd have kept his dignity intact.

She reached across the table and laid her hand, which was soft and small, on top of his. "Asking for help isn't a weakness you need to apologize for, Weston. It's a sign of strength."

He didn't respond—he didn't know how to. When he'd asked for help as a kid, nothing good had ever come from it. He didn't believe anything good would come from it now.

After a moment, she slanted her chin at his pasta. "You done?"

"Yeah."

She stood and reached for his bowl, but he stopped her by picking it up himself. "I'll get it." He took it to the sink. She trailed after him.

"What time do you want to leave for the hospital tomorrow?"

He turned off the water. "Blondie, you don't have to—"

"I want to."

"Even if I can't—"

"Pay me?" she said. "Yep, even then."

"Why?" Everything about this conversation was confusing. He didn't understand her at all.

She smiled at him, but it was a sad smile, a wistful one. "We were friends once, weren't we?"

They'd been more than friends. Yes, they'd been young, and they'd only kissed once, and they hadn't known each other very long at all, but he'd loved her.

"Yeah, we were friends," he said quietly.

"Then let me be your friend now, Weston."

It had been so long since he'd had a real friend. Ever since his mother's death, he'd held himself apart from other people, never wanting them to get close enough to discover the truth about his violent family history, the shame of his past.

He looked at her for a long moment and then he nodded. He had to.

But not for himself.

For Aiden.

Chapter Seven

Irene wanted to visit Mabel in the hospital on Saturday morning, so that's where Chloe and Steve agreed to exchange Aiden.

The hospital reminded Chloe more of a museum than a medical center with its floor-to-ceiling windows, its waterfall fountain and its gleaming tile floors.

"I've told her a million times it's not safe for her to live alone anymore," Irene said, anxiously fingering her pearl necklace as she and Chloe waited for the elevator. "It's a good thing Steve insisted on getting her that medical alert device, otherwise she might still be home on the floor."

Irene was trim and active—both physically and mentally. She walked three miles and did a crossword puzzle every day. She also claimed that "seventy was the new forty," and insisted that having Chloe as a housemate was the equivalent of having "an in-home fountain of youth."

As young as Irene claimed to feel, it was surprising that she was so put off by the fact that Bill Anderson was a few years younger. Was that the real reason Irene was so hesitant? Bill had been steadfast in his pursuit, but how long would he wait? At some point, a man would get tired of waiting and walk away, wouldn't he?

The two women got off the elevator and made their way to Mabel's room. She looked comfortable enough propped up in bed, a vase of Christmas flowers—a mix of white roses and red Hypericum berries—by the window. Steve sat beside her. Aiden was asleep in the baby wrap on his chest.

Irene practically ran to the bed and clutched one of Mabel's hands—the one that wasn't hooked up to the IV—in her own. "Who's going to help me with that Christmas jigsaw puzzle now?"

Mabel chuckled. "Good to see you, too, Irene. Who's watching the store?"

"Brett's not working right now," Irene said. "He offered to step in."

Mabel patted her friend's hand. "He's a good boy." She shot a smile at Steve. "Just like my nephew."

He shifted uncomfortably in his seat. Chloe stifled a giggle, unsure why she found his discomfort so funny. After hearing about his money problems last night, she definitely felt better about leaving the past in the past. So what if she still didn't understand why he'd left without so much as a backward glance eleven years ago? At least he trusted her enough to confide in her now.

Maybe, despite their history, they actually could be friends.

Irene looked at them. "Why don't you two take the baby and go get something to eat? Give me and Mabel a little time for girl talk."

Steve turned to Chloe. He looked very serious. He also looked exhausted. "Are you hungry?"

Chloe shook her head. "I already ate."

"Then how about coffee?" Mabel chimed in.

Steve turned to the older ladies. "Would you like us to bring something back for you?"

Both women demurred. Steve stood, careful not to wake Aiden with any sudden movements, and they made their way into the hall.

"You look tired," Chloe said.

He gave her a wry grin. "Thanks."

"Was Aiden up a lot in the night?"

Steve shook his head. "Just a lot on my mind."

Chloe nodded. "I can imagine."

"You want coffee, Blondie?"

She shrugged. "Not really."

"Then let's go for a walk." He led her to the

elevator, then down to the entrance and out the front door. Past the parking lot was a well-groomed fairway—part of the eighteen-hole championship course next door to the hospital.

Although golf season on the Cape officially ended in October, some courses stayed open as long as there was no snow on the ground. The warm water in Cape Cod Bay meant that winter temperatures here were significantly warmer than elsewhere in Massachusetts, with daytime temps in the forties, although today it felt more like fifty-five—or even sixty. It really was unseasonably warm.

Chloe liked not freezing, but she was still hoping for some Christmas snow.

They stayed next to the woods, in case they needed to duck out of the way quickly should any golfers come through. When they came to a bend in the course, Steve stopped walking. Aiden was still strapped to his chest—awake now, but quiet. Steve had put a little baby hat on his head.

Steve blew into his hands a couple times, looking uncertain. "I think I'm going to sell my house."

Chloe felt her brow furrow. "You're leaving Wychmere Bay?"

"No, but if I can sell it fast enough and find

a decent rental, I'll be able to pay off my credit card debt and make my loan payments."

Chloe bit her lip. One of her mother's old friends was a real estate agent, and Chloe was pretty sure she'd heard the woman talk about how slow the housing market was around the holidays. "How fast would you need to sell it?"

"Within sixty days."

Chloe gave a low whistle. "That's fast."

"I'll price it aggressively. Hopefully get an offer right away."

"But it's such a great house. And you and your sister put so much work into that amazing nursery."

Steve frowned and rubbed the back of his neck. "Desperate times…"

She nodded. "I get it. It's just a shame."

"I don't want you to worry about your paycheck."

Chloe waved her hand. It annoyed her that he thought she was worried about the money. Hadn't they established last night that the paycheck wasn't her priority? If she could help, she wanted to help. She didn't need the quid pro quo. "I'm not worried about that right now."

"Even for this weekend. I might not be able to pay you right away, but I *will* pay you, Blondie. I'm not the kind of guy who shirks his obligations."

"I never said you were."

The expression on his face was both earnest and intense. "You caught me at a bad time last night. I never should have spilled my guts to you that way."

"That's what friends are for, Weston," she reassured him. "I wish you'd let me talk to Pastor Na—"

"I don't think we should be friends." His words came out in a rush.

The stab of pain and confusion she felt caught her off guard. "We shouldn't?"

"You work for me. I'm your employer."

"That doesn't mean—"

"Yes, it does. You shouldn't have to worry about my personal problems. That's not fair to you."

"Cat's already out of the bag on that one," she argued.

"I'm not a charity case. I have a plan."

"A desperate, last-minute plan. Do you really think your house is going to sell that fast over the holidays?"

He set his jaw. "I'll figure it out." His tone was business-like, final. The subtext was clear: *I'll figure it out on my own. I don't need you.*

Again, she felt blindsided by how much his words hurt. He'd only been back in her life for a little over a week. She shouldn't care this much that he didn't want to be friends.

She narrowed her eyes. If Steve was going to cut her out the way he had when they were teens, she at least deserved an explanation this time around. "You said you wanted to be friends."

"*You* said you wanted us to be friends."

It felt like she'd been slapped in the face. It had been her, hadn't it? After everything she'd said to Laura and Brett about this job just being about the money, *she'd* been the one who'd tried to turn it into something else. Maybe her brother was right, and she *was* too nice for her own good.

Was that what had happened when she and Steve were teenagers, too? Had he kissed her that night simply because she'd made herself available? Had he ever had any kind of feelings for her at all?

Well, forget him. If he didn't want her help, if he didn't want her friendship, she wasn't going to force it on him. Let him sell his cottage at a loss. Let him lose his clinic.

"Fine," she snapped. "We're not friends. You're paying me for my babysitting services. I won't concern myself with your personal life. I get it."

The look in his eyes softened. "Blondie, it's not—"

"Don't call me that anymore."

"What? Blondie?" He looked surprised.

"No one's called me that for at least ten years. And even back then, it was just my friends."

Now he looked hurt, and it made her mad. He didn't get to tell her they shouldn't be friends and then get all bent out of shape when she didn't want him to use an old nickname. That wasn't fair to her, either.

"Is Aiden awake?" she demanded.

Steve looked down. "Yes."

"Give him to me."

He gave her a wary look. "If you don't want to watch him today, you don't have to."

"Give. Him. To. Me."

Still looking uneasy, he took the baby out of the wrap and put him in her arms. She winced at the pain in her back as she shifted him up onto her shoulder. Steve looked like he was about to say something about it, but she thrust her chin toward the carrier and said, "The wrap, too."

He untied it and handed it over.

"Are we switching cars or what?" They'd been doing that all week—Steve would drive her car to work so that she'd have access to his car, and the baby's car seat, for her trips to see Mabel.

He rubbed the back of his neck. "I didn't mean to upset you."

She laughed. It came out sounding slightly hysterical. "What did you think was going to happen?"

He flinched. "I don't know. I'm just— I'm bad at this."

"Bad at what?"

He gave her a beseeching look. "Look, if things were different…"

"It is what it is, Weston." She held out her hand, palm up. "Give me your keys and I'll take Aiden home."

He gave an unhappy sigh and handed them over. "I don't know how long I'll have to stay at the hospital."

"It's fine. I know you'll pay me when you're able."

Then she turned on her heel and walked away.

Chapter Eight

It was a good thing Aiden was a mellow baby, because Chloe's emotions were all over the place. One minute she was on the verge of tears and the next she was furious. To distract herself, she clipped Aiden into his bouncy chair and read him stories until it was time for his bottle and a nap.

There was a good library in the nursery with lots of classic children's books. There was even a little set of science board books. She read one to Aiden but didn't find it very engaging and went back to Dr. Seuss, which she could read with lots of expression in her voice.

After he went down for his nap, the doorbell rang. She debated not answering it, but then realized that she had Steve's keys and, if it was him, he might not be able to get in.

It wasn't Steve at the door, though. It was Brett, holding a casserole dish.

"Oh. Hey."

He laughed. "Nice to see you too, sis."

"What are you doing here?"

He raised his eyebrows and lifted the casserole. "What does it look like I'm doing here?"

Whatever was inside smelled fantastic—seafood paella, if Chloe had to guess.

"He won't want it."

Brett gave her a weird look. "Somebody's in a sour mood today."

She shrugged. "He told me he doesn't like 'charity.'"

Her brother laughed again. "Well, too bad. Irene and Nate already have a whole meal train set up. No stopping it now." He moved past her and set the casserole dish on the kitchen counter. "Where's the baby?"

"Sleeping."

"Nice place they've got here."

"Well, hey, by all means, invite yourself in."

His eyebrows furled as he leaned back on the counter and looked at her. "What's the matter?"

"Nothing."

"Is it Dan? Did that creep contact you again?"

She wrapped her arms around her waist. "It's not Dan."

He cocked his head to the side. "Then why so glum, chum?"

"It's nothing."

"Chloe." He stared at her until she started to squirm. "C'mere." Without waiting for her to move, he hooked his giant arm around her shoulders and pulled her in for a hug. He was nearly a foot taller than she was, having inherited their father's tall genes while she'd inherited their mother's short ones. "Tell your big bro what's wrong," he said, giving her hair a hard ruffle.

"Brett!" she squealed. "You're messing up my hair!"

"Like your hair isn't always a mess, anyway. Now, come on. Tell me why you're in such a bad mood."

"It's stupid, okay? Weston told me this morning he doesn't want to be friends with me, and it—it hurt my feelings, that's all."

Brett looked at her for a long moment, then finally said, "Huh."

"Huh, what?"

"When you told me about taking the nanny job, you said you were over him."

She glared at him. "I *am* over him."

"And that this job was just about the money."

"It *is* just about the money."

"Then why do you care if he doesn't want to be your friend?"

She felt her mouth drop open. "Wouldn't *you* care?"

Her brother ran a hand through his shaggy brown hair. If anyone in their family had perennially messy hair, it was him—not her. "Not really. Not if it was someone I didn't really know. You can be friendly without being friends, right?"

She huffed out a frustrated breath. "You're such a guy."

"And *you're* such a girl. But, seriously, it's not a crime if someone doesn't like you, Chloe. And," he said, staving off her protest by holding up his hand, "it's not your job to make them like you, either."

She folded her arms across her chest. "I know that, Brett."

"Do you? 'Cause I'll be honest, I would *never* take a job working for an ex, no matter how badly I needed the money."

She narrowed her eyes. "You just don't want me to leave. You want me to keep working at the restaurant."

"Well, duh. Of course I do. But not at your expense."

"Meaning?"

"Look, sis. I know I pressured you into staying at Half Shell after Mom and Dad died—"

She gave a humorless laugh. "You think?"

"But you didn't exactly lay it all out for me. I knew what I wanted, and I thought that's what you wanted, too. You never said anything about wanting to be a teacher."

To her horror, she felt her eyes fill with tears. "You can want more than one thing at a time, Brett."

He pulled her in for another side hug. "I know you can. I know. But God put that desire to teach in your heart for a reason. Trust in that. Trust in *Him*."

She swiped at the moisture under her eyes. "I hate leaving you in the lurch…"

"Pfft. I'll find another general manager. One who's dreamed about running a restaurant as awesome as Half Shell their whole life. Don't you worry about me. And as for Weston," he said, stepping back and smirking at her, "the guy probably just doesn't want to see you get all lovelorn over him again."

She let out an indignant huff. "I was not lovelorn over him."

"Chloe, please," Brett scoffed. "You cried over him for, like, a month straight."

"In high school."

"And look at you now, all worked up and fuming. Aside from the whole Dan debacle, I haven't seen you this upset about anything in ages. You want me to take back the paella? Tell him to stay away from the Christmas Eve potluck? Make sure I never ask Steve Weston to join us for pizza ever again?"

The way he said it made it sound like a joke, but she knew her brother was serious. Annoying though he could sometimes be, he always had her back. "No, it's fine."

"'Cause I'll do it. Just say the word and I'll snub him good."

She laughed and patted his arm. "Cool your jets, Rambo. I know you would."

"I never could understand why he didn't call you after he left that summer. Kid was obviously head over heels for you, too."

She snorted. "Yeah, right."

He held up his hands. "I'm serious. The guy was quiet, but he practically had little cartoon hearts in his eyes every time he looked at you. Which, as your brother and sworn protector, I can tell you was a lot."

Her eyebrows peaked. "Sworn protector?"

He rolled his eyes. "I'm not joking. Dad made me promise to look out for you that summer."

Chloe sighed. She missed her parents every day. "If you were supposed to look out for me, how come you let me hang out with him?"

"If I thought he was some punk kid looking to take advantage of you, I wouldn't have, but like I said, little cartoon hearts." He made popping gestures with his hands.

She shook her head. "You're ridiculous."

He grinned and cupped a hand behind his ear. "What's that? You think I'm awesome? Why, thank you. I think so, too."

She pushed on his arm. "All right, time to go. If the baby wakes up while you're still here, there won't be room for him with your giant ego taking up all the space."

"The ladies love confidence."

"Introduce me to all these ladies of yours sometime," she said sweetly as she escorted him to the door. She knew full well that her brother hadn't dated anyone since the girl he'd loved in Boston had rejected him when he'd proposed. "I'd love to meet them."

He smirked. "Well played, sis. Well played."

"See you tomorrow at church?"

"You know it," he said, pulling her in for a last, quick hug. "Just remember that you're outta here in a couple weeks anyway. Don't let any of the jokers around here get you down."

"I won't." She waved and shut the door behind him, wishing she could dig into the paella before Steve got home. Brett was an amazing cook, but he was an even better brother. Who else could lighten her mood, tell it to her straight and remind her to trust God all in one fell swoop?

What would happen when she moved to Boston and they didn't see each other all the time anymore?

Honestly, she was dreading it a little. Whenever she and Brett fought when they were growing up, her mom would always remind her, "He's not just your brother—he's your best friend."

It was true, too. Although they argued all the time, Brett loved her unconditionally and understood her like no one else.

If she ever found a man who was even half as supportive as her brother, she'd marry him in a heartbeat. Too bad the only men she'd met lately were liars, like Dan, or guys who'd hurt her, like Steve.

As Steve pulled into his driveway, Brett was heading toward his car. He stopped when he saw Steve and waited for him to get out. Steve's anxiety kicked into high gear.

He'd been happy to see Brett last weekend at church, but now he was worried the guy was going to freeze him out. He deserved it—he knew he did. What kind of person went around telling other people they weren't his friends?

Weirdly, though, Brett didn't look angry. "Hey, how's it going, man? Mabel doing okay?"

Steve smiled over the knot of tension he was feeling. "She's hanging in there."

Brett hitched his thumb toward Steve's house. "I dropped off dinner. Can't guarantee my sister's not gonna throw it in the trash before you get in there, though."

"Uh…thanks."

Brett opened his car door but didn't get inside. "Listen, I don't know what happened between you two back in the day, but she's a sweet girl, and she's had to deal with a lot of nonsense lately, so if you're playing games with her, you'd better cut it out quick."

Steve rubbed the back of his neck. He hadn't been trying to play games—he'd panicked. He didn't get close to other people. He didn't share his problems. And he certainly didn't open himself up for charity—or pity—from beautiful blond women or their pastors and friends.

He'd been up half the night taking care of Aiden, and the other half trying to figure out how to get out from under all his debt. And he'd come up with what had seemed like the perfect solution: sell the cottage. Only, Chloe hadn't seemed terribly impressed with that idea, and she'd still wanted to enlist Pastor Nate's help in getting the whole town involved in his troubles.

Troubles they'd think he deserved if they ever found out what his father had done.

He'd never wanted Chloe to know about that, but at that moment, with Brett giving him such a beady-eyed stare, he knew he had to tell her. And if she didn't want anything to do with him afterward, then so be it. He'd find another nanny.

"I'm not playing games with her, man."

Brett gave him a short nod. "Good."

The other man drove off. Steve stared at the pond. The water was calm today, a murky green-gray. He wondered if it would freeze when it snowed.

He walked up to his front door and tapped on it lightly. When he tried the handle, he found it unlocked. "Hello?" he called out.

Chloe came out of the hallway, stopping well short of where Steve was standing. "I was just checking on Aiden. He's taking a nap." Her voice was pinched.

"That's good," he said, taking a deep breath in an attempt to settle the nerves that were swirling in his stomach.

"I'm going to go now."

"Blo—Chloe. Wait. Can we talk?"

She gave him a tight smile. "I don't think we have anything to talk about."

"I'm sorry about this morning."

"Which part?"

Clearly, she wasn't going to make this easy for him—the apology or the explanation. His heart was beating out of his chest, but if he didn't make things right between them, she was going to quit for sure.

"When I left, back in high school—that wasn't your fault."

She gave him an incredulous look. "Maybe us trying to work together wasn't such a good idea."

He ran his hands through his hair. "I'm messing this up." He paused, trying to formulate exactly what it was he wanted to say. "It's not that I don't *want* to be friends with you, it's just… I don't have a lot of friends. And I freaked out."

Her brow creased. "Freaked out about what?"

He nodded at the kitchen table. "Can we sit?"

She hesitated, then nodded. They sat.

"Um, so you know how I told you my mom's dead and my dad's in prison?"

She nodded.

"He's in prison because he killed her."

Her eyes widened with shock. There was a moment of awkward silence. Finally, she cleared her throat. "I'm so sorry. I…um, I don't know what to say."

"I don't really tell people about it. That's why I didn't try to contact you after I left Cape Cod that summer. It happened the night of that last bonfire. He said it was an accident, that she just fell, but he walked out and he didn't call 9-1-1. My sister was the one who found her. She was never the same."

Chloe had a look of deep concentration on her face, but not horror. He was thankful for that.

"People back home treated us differently after that. He was a drunk, so people had never had much use for him, but afterward…they didn't have much use for me, either."

She sucked in a breath.

"I only had one year left of high school, so we stayed in New Hampshire until I graduated. Aunt Mabel moved in with us to help us. She was there for us during the trial, too."

"I'm sorry." She said it quietly. His nerves were starting to calm down.

"I should have called and told you, back then. You deserved to know. But it was just so overwhelming, and I was so sad and angry and ashamed…" He stared at his hands as he said it. He didn't want to look at her. To see disappointment, or criticism, or scorn.

"It's okay, Steve."

He looked up. She seemed to mean it.

"Really," she said gently. "It's okay."

"Your brother thinks I'm playing games with you. I'm not. It was just…when you started talking about telling other people about the money I owe, I freaked out. I've worked really hard the last ten years, Chloe. Really hard. I want to have a place in the community where I'm respected, not one where people think I'm a charity case or a liability, or where they're worried I might end up like my dad. Can you understand that?"

She nodded. "I do. I understand."

"I don't want people to know. I don't want people to think less of me."

She blew her bangs out of her eyes, which were full of sympathy and compassion. "I understand. I'm glad you told me."

"I'd like to be friends, if you still want that," he said.

"You know you're not in debt because you did something wrong, don't you?"

"I shouldn't have put my emergency fund toward the down payment."

"Would you have been able to afford the clinic otherwise?"

He gave her a wry smile. "I can't afford it now."

She looked out the window. He followed her gaze. The sun had set not long after 4:00 p.m., so it was dark now. The Christmas lights in his trees were shining, little sparks of color symbolizing hope in the night. "Did your sister have a baby shower? For Aiden?"

He shook his head. "It was pretty much just me and her after she got out of rehab. Her old friends were the ones she partied with, so we didn't even let them know she was pregnant."

"Can I throw him one? It wouldn't be charity. People have baby showers for their friends. It's what they do."

"You want to throw Aiden a baby shower?" He felt his lips quirk up.

"Yeah," she said, "I do."

"You're going to keep working for us?"

"Well, I don't know, Weston. That Aiden's a pretty tough taskmaster…"

"I'm really sorry for what I said earlier."

She smiled and gave his hand a little pat. "I know. And I accept your apology."

"Did you throw Brett's dinner in the trash?"

She laughed. "Is that what he told you?"

"It smells really good."

"I didn't ask him to bring it. Apparently, Irene and Nate set up a meal train for you because of Mabel. It wasn't me."

He got up and found the casserole dish. The contents looked as good as they smelled—saffron rice packed with shrimp, clams, mussels and slices of chorizo. He took two bowls out of the cupboard. "You want to stay and eat?"

She shrugged, but she looked pleased. "Sure."

He dished out the food and brought the bowls to the table, along with a glass of water for each of them. They took a moment to pray. He felt incredibly light right now, like he was weightless, knowing that she'd forgiven him for being a jerk earlier. Knowing that she knew about what his father had done and she was still here, still wanted to be his friend.

He took a bite of the paella. "Whoa. This *is* really good."

Chloe lifted an eyebrow. "You doubted Brett's culinary prowess?"

"The guy burned hot dogs like nobody's business."

She grinned. "That was a long time ago."

He took another bite. "Obviously."

After they'd eaten some more, Aiden started crying and they both rose from their seats. "I've got it," Steve said. "You're off the clock."

He took Aiden out of his crib and bounced him up and down to calm him. "You want your bottle, buddy? You hungry?"

He brought him into the family room. Chloe was at the kitchen counter, getting the formula ready. "Top's secure?" he asked.

"That was one time, Weston. Cut me some slack."

He grinned. "Just checking."

He sat in an armchair and Aiden took the bottle immediately. Steve relaxed into the chair, enjoying the warm weight of his nephew in his arms. "How long did he sleep?"

Chloe sat on the couch across from him. "Almost three hours."

Steve sighed. "Why can't he sleep like that at night?"

"Have you heard of the five S's?"

"Nope."

"It's five things to do to soothe fussy babies. Swaddle them. Put them on their side or stomach. Shush them. Swing them or let them suck on something."

"Okay…"

"He likes the wrap because he's swaddled, swinging and listening to the sound of your heartbeat—it probably reminds him of being in the womb. The crib at night is too quiet. Too still."

"Ah," he said. "So they need to invent a rocking crib? Is that it?"

"They actually have them already," she told him. "They're called 'smart cribs,' and one can be yours for the low, low price of twelve hundred dollars."

His eyes bugged out. "Twelve hundred dollars?"

She shrugged. "Technology costs the big bucks. But I'll bring over an exercise ball tomorrow. If you can't go for a walk with him because it's raining or the middle of the night or something, you can sit on the ball and bounce him a bit to calm him down."

"That's genius."

"I take no credit," she said. "I'm simply passing along what I've read."

"I have a million exercise balls at the clinic. You don't need to bring one."

She yawned. "All right."

"Go home, Bl—sorry. Chloe."

"You can call me Blondie. I don't mind."

Aiden finished his bottle, so Steve put him on his shoulder so he could burp him. "Are you sure?"

"We had fun that summer, didn't we? At church camp?" She had a wistful, faraway look in her eyes.

Aiden let out a giant belch and they both laughed. "Yeah, it was fun," Steve said.

"You need anything else before I go?"

"Will you hold him for a second while I put the dishes in the dishwasher?"

"Look at you, getting all fancy and cleaning your own dishes."

He felt heat creep up his neck. The house had been a disaster zone when she'd first seen it. He was embarrassed that she'd had to clean up after him. She probably thought he was a complete slob. "The state of my house when you first saw it isn't how I normally live."

"I know, Weston. I'm just teasing you."

"Really. I can't cook to save my life, but I'm usually pretty decent at picking up after myself."

"You've got more important things on your mind right now," she said, doing a peekaboo face at Aiden. "Don't worry about it."

She held out her hands for the baby, then winced like she had on the golf course when he put Aiden in her arms. "Are you all right? That's the second time today you've made a face when you've taken the baby. Did you hurt yourself?"

"It's just my back. I've got a couple of slipped disks."

He grimaced. "How'd you manage that?"

"Car accident."

He remembered what she'd told him about how her parents had died. "The one…?"

"Yup. That one." She gave him a small, sad smile. "I don't remember much of it, so that's a blessing."

"Did you need back surgery?"

"No."

"Were you hurt anywhere else?"

"I had some cuts and bruises. A mild concussion. Couple of broken ribs. Nothing major."

"And your parents…?"

She was bouncing Aiden, holding him close. "It was a head-on collision. They were in the front."

"I'm so sorry."

She kissed the top of Aiden's head and smoothed

a hand over his hair. "Let's talk about something else. Something happy."

Steve wanted to make her happy more than just about anything in the world. He racked his brain for something light and cheery to say. "Irene brought tea-flavored fudge to the hospital. I didn't care for it that much, but Aunt Mabel loved it."

Chloe nodded. "Yeah, Irene likes to experiment."

"Where does she make it?"

"Still trying to unlock the secrets of The Candy Shack?"

He just looked at her expectantly.

"She makes it in our kitchen. Packages it there, too."

"Do you get to do taste tests?"

She hitched her shoulder like it was no big deal. "Sometimes."

"What's the weirdest flavor of fudge you've tried?"

She was quiet a moment, pondering, several strands of her long blond hair framing her face. *So pretty, and so sweet. So understanding, too.* He wished he had something to offer her. He'd dreamed of her for eleven years, and the reality of spending time with her was even better than he'd imagined. He didn't want their friendship to end when she left for Boston. This time, he'd stay in touch with her for sure.

"Velveeta's pretty weird," she said, "but roast beef's probably the weirdest."

"Roast beef," he repeated, fake gagging. "Are you serious?"

"It doesn't taste like roast beef—it's chocolate-flavored, but the beef cuts the sweetness. You want to try it?" she asked.

"What? Now?"

"No, Weston. Not now," she said. "But maybe tomorrow? After church? If Irene's willing to sit with Mabel at the hospital, I can give you and Aiden the behind-the-scenes tour."

"That'd be cool. Afterward, I can show you the clinic and give you some exercises that might help your back."

"Oh, yeah. I should have thought of that before."

"Okay, let me go throw those dishes in the dishwasher."

He hightailed it into the kitchen and cleaned up.

Amazingly, although it had started out rough, the evening had been the best one he'd had in a very long time.

Chapter Nine

The Candy Shack was closed on Sundays, but when Chloe had let them in, she'd been struck, as always, by the incredible smell: sweet and sugary, with a hint of citrus and chocolate.

Although she lived upstairs, Chloe didn't actually come into the store that often, but when she did, she liked perusing the penny candy bins: those weird marshmallow peanuts, jawbreakers, gumballs and fruit chews. And, of course, the saltwater taffy, Cape Cod's claim to fame, in all sorts of flavors including sea salt, licorice, molasses and caramel swirl.

Irene had given them her permission to be in the store. She was at the hospital with Mabel, and she'd told them she'd stay as late as they wanted, so they should take their time.

That was a good thing, because they'd been here for a while, and Steve was transfixed by the intricate gingerbread town Irene had set up in the window. He was now describing the whole scene to Aiden, who was snuggled up in the wrap.

There was a church with a steeple, several snow-covered houses, and a large gabled house that looked suspiciously like The Sea Glass Inn. There was also a gingerbread train running through the gingerbread town.

"I wonder how long it took Irene to build everything?" Steve marveled. "It had to be so much work."

"She loves it, though," Chloe told him. "Says it keeps her young."

He gave her a sly look. "I thought the fountain of youth was in the roast beef fudge."

Chloe snorted. She'd enjoyed eating the roast beef fudge. He'd totally chickened out. "For someone who wanted to live in a chocolate factory, you don't have much of a sweet tooth."

He laughed and adjusted the way Aiden was sitting in the wrap. "What can I say? I'm not really a dessert person. But it's fun to be here all by ourselves. And watching you eat roast beef fudge? Priceless."

"It was delicious!" she insisted. "I couldn't even taste the beef."

He made a face. "I'll take your word for it."

"You're sure you don't want to try anything

else before we go?" she asked, jingling the keys in her hand.

"I'm good, Blondie. Let's get to the clinic so I can show you those back exercises."

She locked up and they walked down Main Street toward the clinic, passing by a sandwich shop, a kite shop and numerous souvenir shops, as well as Just Duckie, a rubber duck store that had a four-foot-tall Santa duck on display in the window.

"When did that open?" Steve asked, stopping in front of the store.

"Six or seven years ago. Great party favors. I actually just bought a whole bunch of little Cape Cod–themed ducks for my new students. I thought it would be a fun way to introduce myself, since I'll be coming in halfway through the year."

"Yeah, how does that work?" he asked. "Who's teaching them right now?"

"Oh, they have a classroom teacher who's there for the whole year. She'll be my mentor when I get there, and she'll help me plan lessons and give me feedback."

"Ah, so it's like on-the-job training?"

She nodded. "Exactly. It's a teaching internship."

They started walking again. Family Physio

was just down the street. "Will they hire you for real if they like you?"

She shook her head. "It doesn't really work like that for teaching. I mean, maybe if they had an opening for the next year. But it's not like a corporate internship where you're hoping to get your foot in the door at a specific company."

"So, you could go anywhere after your internship's done?"

"Provided I pass, yeah. Anywhere in Massachusetts, at least."

"Do you want to stay in Boston?"

She shrugged. "I'm open to it."

"Even though you've always lived here?"

"You know how small towns are. Sometimes it's good to get a fresh start."

He gave her a funny look. "What do you need a fresh start for? Look at you—you're perfect."

She choked on a laugh. "Yeah, right."

"I'm serious. You're beautiful, smart, a great musician—"

She laughed again, and he gave her a quelling look.

"Plus, you're nice, and you've got great friends. You don't exactly seem like the kind of person who needs a fresh start."

She looked at him for a long moment. He seemed completely serious, which weirded her out. She was definitely far from perfect. "You don't know everything about me, Weston."

"Well, lay it on me, Blondie," he said, patting Aiden's back through the wrap. "You know my big secret. What's yours?"

She looked away. It was one thing to talk about Dan with people who already knew what had happened. It was another thing altogether to tell someone new.

Especially someone who'd just told her she was perfect. And beautiful, too.

Dan had never told her she was beautiful. Not once.

Steve's words were enough to get the butterflies in her stomach swirling, although Chloe honestly didn't think he'd been speaking from a romantic point of view. As they'd discussed last night, they were going to be friends. Nothing more.

"I was seeing this guy over the summer…"

"Hang on," he said, digging his keys out of his pocket and nodding at the door to his clinic. "Let's go inside."

He held the door open for her, then followed her in and flicked on the lights.

It was a large space, a cross between a gym and a doctor's office with its raised beds, rolling stools and various pieces of exercise equipment, including a treadmill, three exercise bikes and a handful of weight machines.

Chloe turned to look at him. "All of this for just you?"

He chuckled. "No, I also have an assistant. One of the things I was most excited about when I bought the place was that there's plenty of room to expand and grow the practice." He pulled Aiden out of the wrap and handed him to her so he could untie the fabric. "Now, of course, I wish I'd gone smaller."

"It's not over 'til it's over," Chloe said, taking off Aiden's little hat and smoothing the dark, silky hair on his soft little head.

"Uh-huh," Steve said absently. "So, tell me more about this guy."

She blew a raspberry. "I was hoping you'd gotten distracted."

"Must've been serious if you're leaving town over it."

She wished it had been as serious for Dan as it had been for her. "It was a whirlwind thing. Met him on a dating app, went out a few times, then he started talking about the future. I thought he was joking at first, but Laura and Jonathan had just fallen in love really fast, and Dan was so enthusiastic about it, he kind of pulled me in."

Thinking about it now, she realized he'd been all charm, no substance. When Chloe finally met the man God intended her to marry, she'd know it because their relationship would go beyond the surface level. They'd share their real fears and insecurities. They'd be open about their vulnerabilities. It wouldn't all be flash and charm.

Steve had a little furrow between his eyes. "Okay, so he swept you off your feet, but then…?"

"But then I found out he was seeing someone else at the same time."

He winced. "Ouch."

Talking about it still felt humiliating. She'd assumed that she and Dan were on the same page about their relationship, but obviously she'd been dead wrong about that. "They got married less than a month after he broke up with me."

"What a jerk," Steve said. He rummaged in the diaper bag he'd been carrying and pulled out Aiden's change pad, wipes and a fresh diaper, then set everything up on one of the raised beds. "Do they live here in Wychmere Bay?"

Chloe laid the baby on top of the change pad and unzipped his pajamas. "No. He was from Newport, so a couple hours' away. But still. Everyone here knows what a fool I was."

Steve switched out Aiden's wet diaper for the dry one. "I'm sorry, Blondie. And you had no idea he was seeing the other woman?"

"None. I actually should've been doing my student teaching placement this semester, but he asked me to put it off so we could see where our relationship was heading, so I did."

He ran a hand over his jaw. "You didn't."

"I thought we were going to get married, Weston. I thought he was 'the one.'"

"No guy who really loves you would ask you to give up your dreams for him."

She sighed. "He didn't ask me to give them up. He asked me to wait a little. And love means compromise, doesn't it? Isn't that what love is? Sacrificing what we want for the good of the other person?"

He shook his head. "Yeah, but not if it's a one-way street. And call me old-fashioned, but I think the guy should be the one to make the big sacrifices, at least up front. That's why he's the one who buys the engagement ring, right? To show the woman he loves that she's more important to him than his hard-earned savings."

Chloe tucked a strand of hair behind her ear, surprised that Steve's view of things was so clear-cut. It was attractive, to be honest. Made her see him in a whole new light. "I always thought an engagement ring was more a symbol than a sacrifice."

"I guess it's both. Unless the guy's independently wealthy," he said, grinning, "in which case, easy come, easy go."

She laughed. "So you're saying I shouldn't set my sights on landing a rich husband?"

He sobered. "This ex-boyfriend of yours. Did he have money?"

She shrugged. "He liked going out for fancy dinners. And he did buy me some expensive gifts."

She saw a muscle in Steve's jaw tighten. He obviously didn't like the way Dan had treated her one bit.

She tapped her foot and looked up at the ceiling. Brett felt the same way Steve did, that everything that had happened had been Dan's fault, but Chloe couldn't help wondering if there was something she'd missed. Some sign that would have clued her in faster, if only she hadn't been so desperate to finally—*finally*—be in love.

Steve nodded down at Aiden. "You mind watching him while I wash my hands?"

She rolled the little guy onto his front for some tummy time, careful to keep her hands on either side of him to make sure he stayed on the table. Babies his age couldn't roll over yet, but they could still squirm.

When Steve came back, he said, "Should I not have asked about this? You look upset."

"I should've known, shouldn't I?"

He made a face. "What were you supposed to do? Run a background check before you went out with the guy?"

"That's not a bad idea. Maybe next time I will."

"Why are you dating guys you meet on dating apps, anyway?"

She arched an eyebrow. "It's a small town, Weston. Slim pickings."

He arched his eyebrow right back at her.

"What? You've never been on any dating apps?"

He put Aiden on his shoulder and rubbed the baby's back. "Not my thing."

"So, how do *you* meet potential dates?"

"I haven't been on a date in a long time."

She snorted.

"I *haven't*."

She still didn't believe him. A good-looking guy like him? Why wouldn't he be dating?

"How come?" she challenged.

"The kind of women I'm interested in aren't looking for a guy like me."

Her eyes bugged out. "What kind of women are you interested in?"

He started laughing. "You should see your face right now. I promise, it's not what it sounds like."

"Most women I know would be happy to go out with someone like you," she admitted.

"Someone like me?"

She just shook her head. "Stop fishing for compliments. You're as bad as Brett."

"Fine. Most women are looking for something long-term, something that's going to lead to marriage, and that's not me."

She felt her eyes go wide again. "You don't want to get married?"

He laughed again. "I'm shocking the socks off you this afternoon, aren't I?"

"Just answer the question. Why don't you want to get married?"

"Uh, you do remember what we talked about last night, don't you? My mom, my dad, prison, the morgue?"

She waved that away. What had happened to his mother was an absolute tragedy, but letting it rule his life? That was a tragedy, too. "You're not your dad, Steve."

"Maybe not, but I've got half his DNA."

"That doesn't mean you're doomed to have an unhappy marriage."

He hitched his shoulder, a weird little half grin on his face, as though he'd given this a lot of thought and nothing was going to change his mind. "Why take the chance?"

She sighed. She could understand the sentiment. Hadn't she done the exact same thing with dating after her first bout of depression?

Avoided it entirely, so that she wouldn't fall into the same kind of black hole she'd fallen into over seventeen-year-old Steve Weston ever again? "Nothing I say's going to make any difference, is it?"

He grinned wider. "Nope."

"Okay, then. Moving on. Show me what I need to do for my back."

They put Aiden on a blanket next to the exercise mats and Steve went through a whole bunch of stretches and core-strengthening exercises with Chloe. He'd debated doing a hands-on exam but decided against it. They were alone in the clinic and he didn't want to make her uncomfortable.

Plus, the fact that she'd just told him that most of the women she knew would be happy to go out with someone like him was playing on a loop in his head, and he couldn't help but wonder if *she* would be happy to go out with someone like him.

Or, more precisely, him. Period.

Before he'd told her he didn't want to get married, of course. Because based on the way she'd reacted, that was obviously a deal breaker for her.

As it should be. She was special, and she deserved the best. A husband, kids and a white picket fence—all of it.

That two-timing ex of hers had clearly done a number on her, but some other man would come along and snap her up. Steve had meant what he'd said to her earlier: she was beautiful and smart and generous and funny and understanding. And, aside from the times they'd argued, she was very relaxing company. When he was around her, his anxiety wasn't nearly so bad.

You're not your dad, Steve.

She'd been interested in him before, when they were kids. If circumstances were different, maybe she'd be interested in him now, too. But circumstances weren't different, so he needed to put a lid on those kinds of thoughts.

"How many more of these do I have to do?" Chloe asked, panting. She was doing an exercise called "the dead bug," where she lay on her back, keeping her lower back pressed into the floor as she raised and lowered her opposite arms and legs.

"Five more on each side," Steve said. The stronger her core muscles, the less strain on her back.

"I can't do any more. I'm shaking."

"You can do it, Blondie. Keep your back pressed into the floor and dig deep. Push." As a physical therapist, part of his job was diagnostic and part of it was motivational. It always gave him a lot of satisfaction to help people do things they hadn't thought possible before.

"You're going to kill me," she panted, her eyes flaring when she realized what she'd said. She stopped moving. "Oh, I didn't mean—"

"It's okay," he said mildly. "I know what you meant."

From the blanket, Aiden started to fuss, and Steve was glad for the distraction. He knew Chloe hadn't meant anything hurtful by what she'd said, but her horrified reaction just highlighted how much his father's actions would always impact any relationship Steve wanted to have.

No woman would ever be able to fully relax around him. In the back of her mind, she'd always wonder if he was capable of doing the same thing as his dad.

And what if she wanted to have children? He knew there were all kinds of debates about nature versus nurture, but what woman would want to take that chance?

His college girlfriend certainly hadn't. And she hadn't been shy about telling him that no one else would, either.

He tightened his hold on the baby. He'd been content to be alone for so long. Why was all of this coming up now?

"Was there more you wanted to show me?" Chloe asked. "Because I don't think I can take any more."

Aiden was still fussing, so Steve flipped him

onto his stomach for tummy time. "Let's do some push-ups with this guy."

"Um, not sure he's ready for push-ups just yet."

Steve got down on his stomach, nose to nose with his nephew. He wanted to get his mind off all these intense feelings he was having for Chloe, who was leaving town any minute now and would never see him as more than a friend.

"That's right, man," he told Aiden. "Lift that head up. I know it's heavy, but the muscles won't grow if you don't work them." Then he did a push-up. "Here. My neck muscles are pretty strong, but I'll do some exercises, too, if it'll make you feel better."

Chloe stifled a giggle. "Show-off."

Aiden let out an indignant little cry. Steve looked at his watch. "One more minute, bud."

"Are you timing tummy time?"

Steve smiled at her. "Of course."

She pulled out her phone and navigated to the stopwatch. "How many push-ups can you do in a minute?"

"Sixty. Easy."

She held out her phone so he could see her press the start button. "Okay, then. Go."

He started immediately, arms and legs stick-straight, up-down, up-down, nose to the floor.

Aiden started to cry at the thirty-second mark, and Chloe put her phone down to pick him up.

When the timer went off, Steve had completed sixty-three push-ups. He hopped to his feet. He could do push-ups all day. "Your turn."

"I'm holding the baby," she protested.

He plucked Aiden out of her hands.

"No fair," she pouted.

"How many can you do?"

"I don't know. I've never tried."

His eyebrow shot up. "You've never done a push-up?"

"I've never timed myself doing push-ups."

"Take a guess," he said, bouncing Aiden to keep him calm.

"I don't know. Ten? But the ones where you push from your knees instead of your toes."

Steve smirked and shook his head in mock disappointment. "Lightweight."

"Braggart."

"I bet you can do fifteen."

"All right, I'll try." She rubbed her hands together. "Knee push-ups, though."

"Knee push-ups," he concurred.

She got in position on the floor and reset her timer. "And…go!" Steve said as she pressed Start.

She dipped once, twice—but she was only going about halfway down.

"Lower, Blondie. Your face should almost touch the floor."

She spread her arms out to give herself more leverage.

"Keep your elbows in line with your body. You don't want to injure yourself."

She brought her arms back in, and he could see that she was struggling. She couldn't get her face anywhere close to the ground.

Steve stooped to pause the stopwatch on her phone. "Try a wall push-up," he said, motioning for her to stand.

"A wall push-up?"

"You know, push-ups against the wall. They're easier for beginners. Exact same thing, except gravity won't be pulling on you so hard, so it'll be easier to maintain the proper form."

"I totally am a lightweight," she said, breathless and laughing.

"Everybody's got to start somewhere. You think I could just drop and do sixty push-ups out of nowhere? I do them every day."

Her eyes widened, and his chest puffed up. Maybe he *had* been showing off for her. And she actually seemed impressed. "Every day?"

He nodded toward the baby. "Well, this guy's messed up my normal routine lately, but usually I get up, spend some time reading the Bible, then do some stretches and strength training before I start my day."

"You don't go to the gym?"

"You don't need all kinds of fancy gym equipment to get a great workout."

She laughed. "Who *are* you?"

He grinned. "The guy who's going to get your back pain under control and help you do a real push-up before you leave for Boston in January."

"All right, Weston," she said. "But only if we exercise together. Because I can tell you right now I'm one of the least self-motivated exercisers you'll ever meet."

A sense of warmth spread through him. She wanted his help—he could *help* her. Not just pay her for babysitting Aiden, but give her something of value that she couldn't get anywhere else.

Maybe he did have something to offer her, after all.

"Sure, Blondie. Just come over to my house ten or fifteen minutes earlier than usual, and we'll go through your routine before I leave for work."

"You going to show me that wall push-up?" she asked, looking a little disheveled.

"Tomorrow," he said, shifting Aiden from one arm to the other. "We need to go liberate Irene from the hospital."

She chuckled and let him lead the way to the exit. "Liberation ahoy!"

Chapter Ten

Irene did not need to be liberated. She was a happy participant in the Christmas party that was going strong in Mabel's room.

Or at least that's what it seemed like to Chloe. In addition to Irene and Mabel, there were a couple other elderly widows and widowers crowded into the room, drinking Christmas punch, eating fruitcake and laughing loudly while exchanging white elephant gifts.

Bill Anderson had just unwrapped a pair of gaudy snowman earrings that he was holding up and showing off like a game show model.

"Very you, Bill," Chloe said, grinning, her eye on the fruitcake, which had the white marzipan icing she loved so much.

Steve, on the other hand, stopped dead in the doorway. "Um, does the hospital allow this many visitors in the room at the same time?"

Bill smiled and waved Chloe and Steve inside. "Come on in, kids. Have some punch."

Chloe slipped past Steve and poured them each a cup from the pitcher resting on the windowsill. As she walked back to Steve, she took a sip. It was perfect—a light and fizzy mix of cranberry juice, orange juice, pomegranate juice and ginger ale. "Oh, wow. Who made the punch?"

Sarah Jenkins, the owner of the British-themed B and B on Main Street, shyly raised her hand. "Try the cookies, dear. I made the Linzer ones you like."

Sarah's shortbread cookies were amazing. "The ones with raspberry jam and powdered sugar?"

Sarah nodded.

Chloe piled up a little paper plate with cookies, fruitcake and Nantucket cranberry pie, one of her brother's specialty desserts.

"Aunt Mabel," Steve said, shifting Aiden higher on his shoulder. "Shouldn't you be resting?"

Mabel made a scoffing noise. "I've been stuck in bed for the last two days and I'm going under the knife tomorrow, Steven. Don't be a party pooper. Let us have our fun."

Aiden squawked, and the older folks all laughed.

"Even the little fella agrees," Bill said, coming to take a closer look.

Steve took Aiden off his shoulder and held

him in his arms so Bill could see him better. "Guess so."

"Handsome little guy." Bill gave Steve a sly grin. "Must take after his uncle."

Steve smirked. "Thanks."

"Oh," Sarah cooed, coming closer. "Look at him! Those tiny hands! Those tiny feet! That tiny nose!" As she reached over to stroke the baby's cheek, Aiden let out a loud cry.

"Those big lungs!" Bill added, waggling his salt-and-pepper eyebrows, and everybody laughed again.

"I think he's hungry," Steve said.

"Want me to take him?" Chloe asked through a big bite of fruitcake.

Steve gave her loaded plate a pointed look. "How about you make the bottle, and then I'll give it to him so you can finish your treats," he suggested, sliding the diaper bag from his shoulder to the floor.

Chloe put down her desserts to pick up the bag. "Sure."

"Look at you two," Irene said. "Such a good team."

Chloe blushed. She and Steve did seem to work well together, but Irene's tone made it sound like there was a lot more to it than that.

Sure, they were friends now, but that's all they were. Even if she finally understood why he'd never called her after that incredible kiss all those years ago. And it wasn't because the guy was a jerk.

But there was no room for romance between them now. Steve didn't want to get married, and she was leaving for Boston soon.

Besides, being friends was good. Who couldn't use more friends?

And surely their teenage kiss hadn't actually been as amazing as she remembered. Memories were unreliable, and she'd been so young. If he kissed her now, it would probably be a total letdown.

Right. And what about that kiss on the cheek under the mistletoe last weekend? Was that a letdown, too?

Chloe gave her head a little shake. Rehashing the way she'd felt under the mistletoe wasn't going to lead anywhere productive. Best to stop thinking about it at all.

The conversation carried on around her as she made Aiden's bottle. Sarah was telling a funny story about one of her great-grandchildren, and then Bill chimed in with a funny story about Hayden.

When the bottle was ready, Chloe handed it to Steve, and he left the room to feed Aiden somewhere quieter and less distracting. She picked up her plate of desserts and took another bite of fruitcake. She didn't care what anybody said about it: fruitcake was the *best*.

Mabel motioned her over, patting the side of her bed in an invitation for Chloe to sit. "Do you like my new footwear?" the older lady asked, pointing to her toes, which were encased in furry cat slippers.

Chloe giggled. "Those are so cute!"

"Irene brought them for the white elephant exchange."

"I love it that your friends organized a hospital party for you."

Mabel smiled and patted Chloe's hand. "When you get to our age, you realize that you've got to cherish every moment. When the Lord says it's my time to go, I'll go gladly, but until then, I'm going to surround myself with the people I love." She picked up her cup of punch from her bedside table and took a shaky sip before setting it down again. "And speaking of the people I love," she said, "Steven's a lot happier since you started watching Aiden."

"I'm glad to help."

Mabel looked out the window, massaging her swollen knuckles, then gave Chloe a weak smile. "He wanted me to move into an assisted living home. Maybe I should have listened, but those places, they just seem so soulless."

Chloe felt bad for her. It had to be hard, get-

ting older with next to no family to help you.
"It's a big decision."

"When he and Eloise told me they were moving to Wychmere Bay, it was such a nice surprise. I never married, you know. They're my
only family."

Chloe patted Mabel's arm. "I know he's glad
to be here for you."

"I hate to cause him more trouble. That boy
has had nothing but trouble since the day he
was born. And with the parole hearing coming
up, this is absolutely the last thing he needs."

Chloe sat straighter at that. Steve's mom had
only died eleven years earlier. Wouldn't his father have to serve more time in prison? Why
would he be up for parole so soon?

Not feeling it was her place to ask about it,
she said, "You're no trouble, Mabel. You're his
family."

"And you're a gift, sweetheart. An answer
to prayer."

Chloe looked up to make sure Steve and
Aiden hadn't reappeared. "Hey, I want to organize a baby shower for Aiden. Do you want
to help me plan it? It would be fun, and it would
give you something to do while you're recuper-
ating from your surgery."

Mabel's eyes lit up. "Of course I want to help.
Does Steven know about it? Is it a surprise?"

"Well, I told him I wanted to organize one, but I didn't tell him when or where or anything, so we can make it a surprise if you want."

"Oh, I love surprises!"

Irene glanced over. "What surprise?"

"We're planning a surprise baby shower for Aiden," Mabel told her. "Maybe we can even do it on Christmas or Christmas Eve!"

"Perfect," Irene said. "Count me in." She turned to her compatriots. "How about you, Sarah? Bill? Would you like to help?"

"Help with what?" Steve asked, standing in the doorway, Aiden in his arms.

Mabel, Irene and Sarah's eyes flickered with alarm. Bill chuckled as Irene said, "Oh, nothing," and Steve gave them all a suspicious look.

Aiden spat up on his shoulder, distracting him, and Chloe jumped off the bed and pulled a burp cloth out of the diaper bag. "Here."

Steve handed her the baby, took the burp cloth and dabbed at his shoulder. "Thanks."

A nurse stopped by a few minutes after he'd cleaned up and informed everyone that the hospital's "quiet hours" were starting soon. They packed up, and everyone except Steve and Aiden left a few minutes later.

As Chloe and Irene got into Irene's car, the older woman asked, "So, how was your afternoon with Steven? He seems like such a nice young man."

"It was good," Chloe said noncommittally. "He gave me some exercises to do for my back."

"Has it been acting up again?"

"I think it's from carrying the baby."

Irene nodded as she started the car. "That baby is sweet as pie." She darted a glance at Chloe. "And I'm sure Steven is doing a great job, but babies need a mother."

"Mmm-hmm," Chloe said, noncommittal again. "Know who else seems sweet? Bill Anderson."

"Oh, pshaw," Irene replied, one hand on the wheel, the other patting her perm. "Don't change the subject, missy."

Chloe smiled and leaned back, grateful that her stint in the hot seat was over and she didn't have to examine her feelings for Steve in greater detail.

Mabel's surgery went well, and Chloe—and Aiden—spent hours with her in the hospital over the next week, discussing the theme and décor for the baby shower.

Chloe was excited because Laura had agreed to host it at The Sea Glass Inn on Christmas Day, which meant she and Brett wouldn't be alone on Christmas. Plus, what better way to celebrate the birth of Baby Jesus than to bless a motherless newborn with the gifts and supplies he'd need?

In the end, she and Mabel decided that they wouldn't need much in the way of shower decorations—the inn was already decked out for Christmas, so they'd just add a banner and some balloons. That way, they could put more money toward presents, and hopefully ease a bit of Steve's financial strain.

He was clearly still struggling, because the For Sale sign for the cottage on Frog Pond had gone up earlier that week.

On Saturday morning, Chloe headed to The Baby Boutique to see if she could find a suitable party banner for the shower. It was one week before Christmas, and although there was still no snow on the ground, the weather had cooled, and she had high hopes that winter would come to Wychmere Bay before the twenty-fifth.

She looked up after she stepped into the store. The mistletoe was still hanging overhead.

Steve had spent fifteen minutes each morning this week helping her with her back exercises. Since they'd cleared the air about why he hadn't called her after their kiss back in high school, they'd had fun together. They made each other laugh.

She wasn't in the market for anything more

than friendship, though. She was leaving in just two weeks.

"Oh, look!" a woman cried out from deeper in the store. Chloe could only see the top of her head over the racks. She was tall and had beautiful red curls. "Don't you just love this baby romper? It's adorable!"

"Honey," the man with her replied. He was even taller, and he had dark, chestnut-colored hair like Dan's. "It's six hundred dollars."

"But feel it," the woman insisted. "It's so soft. Give me your wallet, Danny. I'm buying it."

Chloe started to get a bad feeling, but before she had a chance to turn around and leave, the man sighed and said, "Fine."

The two of them stepped out from behind the racks and Chloe's stomach dropped. The guy didn't just have hair *like* Dan's—he *was* Dan. What on earth was Dan doing back in Wychmere Bay?

Chloe whipped around to hightail it out of there, but Dan's voice stopped her before she could push her way out the door. "Chloe? Is that you?"

She slowly turned to face him. "Hey, Dan."

He strode toward her, all easy smiles and clean-cut charm. "Oh, wow! Good to see you! I was wondering if we'd run into you. What a small world!"

Good to see you? What a small world? Was he for real?

When he'd broken up with her, when he'd told her he was marrying someone else, he'd said he wanted to stay friends. She'd been too shocked to say anything, although Brett thought she should have stood up for herself and told him that with friends like him, she wouldn't need enemies.

Dan motioned to the redhead, who was obviously pregnant. "This is my wife, Marissa." Then he slid his arm around her. "And this is that old girlfriend I was telling you about, babe. Chloe."

The women gave each other tight smiles as they exchanged greetings. Why had Chloe run out the door wearing flannel pants, running shoes and zero makeup? Although she definitely didn't want Dan back, it would have been nice to make him feel like he'd missed out on something.

Instead, she was just *that old girlfriend.* She doubted Dan ever had to tell his gorgeous, pregnant wife to change her clothes, fix her hair or put on high heels before they went out. Marissa was a knockout, and they looked perfect together.

No wonder he never told you that you *were beautiful. Look who he was comparing you to the entire time.*

"Here for some shopping?" Chloe asked, trying to tamp down the hurt she was feeling.

"Here for the holidays," Dan replied, making Chloe's stomach sink all over again. "I knew 'Ris would love this little town."

"It's so…quaint," Marissa said, the compliment not sounding like a compliment at all.

"We're about to check into that beachfront inn your friend owns. What's it called, babe?"

"The Sea Glass Inn."

"Right. The Sea Glass Inn." He smiled at Chloe as though she should be delighted by the news. "We're here until New Year's."

They had to be joking, right? They were staying at her best friend's inn?

If she'd needed any confirmation of Dan's lack of character, she had it now. The guy was as clueless as they came.

Marissa pressed Dan's wallet back into his hand and peered up at him through her eyelashes. "Danny, will you go buy me that baby romper? I need some air."

"Of course." He kissed his wife's cheek then nodded at Chloe. "Nice to see you, Chlo. Maybe we'll see you around."

"Maybe," Chloe mumbled.

Marissa rubbed her pregnant belly while shooting daggers at Chloe with her eyes. When

Dan reached the register, she hissed, "Stay away from my husband. We're having a baby."

Chloe wouldn't touch Dan with a ten-foot pole. "I don't want your husband."

Marissa snorted. "I know he was seeing you last summer before we got engaged. I wanted to come down here and make sure you understood that it's over between you two. He's mine now—we're married. You're never getting him back."

"I already told you, I don't want anything to do with him," Chloe replied crossly.

The corner of Marissa's lip curved up in a sneer. "As if someone like *you* could ever do better than Dan."

"Excuse me?" Chloe shot back. What right did this woman—this *stranger*—have to say something like that to her?

She wasn't going to let her shock get the better of her *this* time around. "Oh, I can do *way* better than the two-timing man you married. In fact, I'm already seeing someone way better. And you can see him with your own two eyes at the Christmas Eve potluck at The Sea Glass Inn."

With that, she thrust the door open and stormed onto the street, horrified at the lie she'd told but also strangely exhilarated that she'd stood up for herself and prevented Dan's wife from getting the last word.

The exhilaration wore off quickly, though, as soon as Chloe realized that the other woman's rudeness had probably come from a place of insecurity rather than spite. If you married someone who'd been unfaithful before the wedding, of course you'd be anxious about his loyalty afterward, as well.

From that perspective, maybe the lie she'd blurted out in anger had actually been a kindness—it would prevent Marissa from worrying that Chloe wanted to get back together with Dan.

But who could she ask to pretend to be her boyfriend? Jonathan was engaged to Laura, and Brett's single friends might get the wrong idea.

Steve wouldn't get the wrong idea, though. The two of them already spent tons of time together, they were both planning on attending the potluck, and they'd been clear about the fact that they were just friends.

Would he help her? Maybe she should simply let her falsehood come to light, but the thought of having to talk to Dan and Marissa again all on her own made her stomach hurt.

She'd come clean to Steve about the lie, and if he didn't want to help her, she'd tell Dan and Marissa the truth and suffer through the fallout—even if it ruined Christmas for everyone involved.

Chapter Eleven

Steve wasn't expecting any guests, so he was surprised to open the door and find Chloe on his doorstep. She was holding a box of pizza that she immediately shoved into his hands.

"Uh, hello." He'd been snoozing on the couch while Aiden napped, and he was feeling a little groggy. "Did we have plans?"

"I did something stupid," she said, looking miserable, her shoulders hunched in her big blue sweater as though she wanted it to swallow her whole.

"Okay…" Trying to shake off any lingering bleariness, he led the way into his house and deposited the pizza on his kitchen counter.

Chloe looked around. "Where's Aiden?"

"Sleeping."

She let out a long breath, opened her mouth

as though she was going to say something, but then lost her nerve.

"You okay?"

She chewed on her lip, giving him a darting, assessing look.

"What's going on?" he asked. "You're making me nervous."

"I ran into my ex-boyfriend this morning."

"The married guy?"

She nodded.

Steve's stomach muscles clenched. "Where?"

"At The Baby Boutique. With his wife."

He scratched his ear. "I thought they lived in Newport?"

Her chin wobbled and her dark eyes filled with tears. "They're here in town for Christmas. And they're staying at The Sea Glass Inn."

"What?"

She looked away. "He seemed totally oblivious that it might bother me, but she's got it in for me, Weston. She thinks I want to steal her man."

"But that's ridiculous…isn't it?" he asked, suddenly feeling unsure.

"It's completely ridiculous," she said. And then she burst into tears.

"Blondie," Steve said helplessly, putting his hand on her elbow and steering her to the couch in the family room. "Please don't cry."

She cried harder after she sat and then angrily

wiped at the tears on her cheeks. "I'm so mad at myself right now."

"Believe me. You're not the one you should be mad at."

"I feel like the world's biggest loser."

"You're not a loser," he said, giving her an awkward pat on the shoulder. What he really wanted to do was to pull her into his arms and hold on tight.

"This Christmas was going to be so special, and now they've ruined it!"

"Hey, come on. You can't let them spoil Christmas."

"Did you know he's the only boyfriend I've ever had? A cheating, lying *liar*."

"The only...?" he repeated, like an idiot. Because how had she never had another boyfriend? She was so beautiful, it was like she'd just stepped out of a fairy tale, and one of the best people he'd ever met to boot.

"And now he's made me a liar, too."

He felt his brow wrinkle. "What do you mean?"

"Know how I told you I did something stupid?"

He nodded.

"I told his wife I was seeing someone to get her to back off."

"That sounds smart to me."

"You might not think so much longer." She twisted her hands in her lap. "I need someone to play the part while they're in town, and my only real option is you."

Steve blinked at her. "You want them to think you're seeing *me*?"

He sounded so incredulous, it made her cringe. Was the idea of dating her really so inconceivable? "I'm sorry. I didn't mean to drag you into this. She was just so rude to me, and you're the only person I can think of who can help."

"What did she say to you?"

She dropped her eyes to her hands. Maybe Steve wouldn't think what Dan's wife had said to her was that bad. Maybe he'd think she was blowing it out of proportion.

"Chloe." He touched her chin, forcing her eyes up. "What did she say?"

She suddenly became aware of the heat of him, the strength of him, the smell of his aftershave so clean and fresh it was like gravity pulling her toward the sun.

"Just that 'someone like me' would never be able to do better than her fine specimen of a husband," she mumbled.

His forehead creased and he stared at her for a long moment. "Does she think she won some kind of prize?"

Chloe huffed out a laugh. He got it! "Exactly! I think I can do a lot better than some guy who was cheating on me with her."

"Guys like that, they don't change," he said earnestly. "My dad did a lot of things wrong, but the fact that he ran around on my mother caused most of the problems in our house."

She put her hand on his arm. "I'm sorry, Weston." It was hard for her to relate. Her parents had had a great marriage—the kind of marriage she wanted to have someday. "How do you know he was cheating on her?"

Steve's shoulders slumped. "He was gone a lot. He went to jail for a bar fight when I was seven, and then again when I was in middle school, for drugs. But there were lots of nights in between that he didn't come home. They'd fight and my mom would cry about it, and then they'd start yelling, and then…" He trailed off, took a breath.

"I called the police a few times, but she'd deny it and refuse to press charges. And then they'd get mad at me."

Chloe sucked in a breath. "Steve," she said, not sure she wanted to know the answer to her question. "Did he hurt *you*?"

He rubbed his forearm. "He broke my arm once, when I was ten, but mostly he just yelled. Once I got to middle school, I basically lived at my friend Liam's house. I think his parents suspected something was…not quite right at home, but after those failed attempts to get the police involved, I never really told anyone else."

Her heart felt so heavy, it literally hurt, a physical ache. "I'm so sorry."

He shrugged, but his eyes were unfocused, as though he were lost in his own world. "I used to replay it over and over. What would have happened if I'd done a better job protecting her. If I'd told Liam's parents. Or a teacher. Or stayed home that summer instead of coming here to Cape Cod."

He scraped his hand against his stubble and she could hear the rasp. "If I'd just done one thing differently, Blondie, just one little thing, I could have saved her life."

She shook her head fiercely, brushing away a tear that had trickled onto her cheek. In trying to comfort her, Steve had opened himself up to so much pain. "No," she said, wanting to shake him, wanting to shake that useless, pointless thought right out of his head. "No."

He glanced at her, and it seemed to snap him out of his head. "I made you cry again."

She wiped away her tears. "You did the best you could, Steve. You were a kid. It wasn't your job to protect her; it was your parents' job to protect *you*."

"I know, but—"

"Did you ever talk to anyone about it? A professional, I mean?"

He gave her a wry smile. "Maybe I should, huh? It was eleven years ago. You'd think I'd be over it by now."

"I don't think there's a timeline for healing grief and trauma," she said earnestly. "I went to therapy after my parents died. I still do. You know there's no shame in asking for help, don't you?"

"For you, maybe."

"For anyone." She looked up at him. His eyes were very blue. "We all need help sometimes, Weston. We can't do this life alone."

He shook his head. "I shouldn't have said anything."

"No, I'm glad you told me."

They were quiet for a moment and then Steve said, "I look just like him, you know. Sometimes I worry that—"

"Don't even finish that sentence. That's the most ridiculous thing I've ever heard."

He chuckled softly. "You don't know what I was going to say."

"Oh, yes, I do. And you are nothing like your dad."

"You don't know that, Blondie. You never met him."

"But I know you, and you're probably the least selfish person I've ever met."

"Am I?"

The fact that he seemed genuinely perplexed by that statement frustrated her. "You gave up your whole life to move down here with your sister, spent all your savings buying a business so you could support her and her son. Then, when she died, you took him in without question and spent money you didn't have on her funeral. Now you're taking care of your injured great-aunt. Which part of that sounds selfish to you?"

His face lit up with a genuine smile. "You really think I'm one of the least selfish people you know?" he asked, his smile making her feel sparkly and alive in a way she'd never experienced before.

That scared her—she couldn't be having feelings for Steve Weston again. He'd already broken her heart once, and he'd told her straight-up that he didn't want to get married. She pushed her emotions down and narrowed her eyes at him in mock agitation. "You're fishing for compliments again, Weston."

He laughed and moved on. "Seriously, though. That guy did you a favor when he broke up with you."

It took her a moment to mentally switch gears back to Dan and Marissa. Their presence seemed trifling now, in light of what Steve had shared. "I know. I just don't want her ruining the Christmas Eve potluck. This might be my last Christmas on Cape Cod, and I want to enjoy it. That's why I told her I was seeing someone. I thought maybe, if she saw us together, she'd get the message and drop it."

"Oh, she'll get the message," Steve said darkly. "But do me a favor. Define *together*."

She brushed her bangs out of her eyes. "You know, like dating together."

"You want to go on a date with me?" he asked, and although she could tell he was teasing her, because of what she'd experienced when he'd smiled a second ago, she felt more vulnerable about this whole situation than she had before.

"I don't mean we'd actually have to go on a date. Just look like we're dating at the potluck. And maybe when we're out around town together. Like at church or whatever."

"How are we supposed to make it look like we're dating when we're at church?"

He was laughing at her. What had she been thinking? "This was a bad idea. I'm sorry."

He put his fingers under her chin and turned her face back to his. "It's not bad. I just want to make sure I understand what you're looking for. How we'll sell it."

Now she felt nervous again, unsettled, with

him sitting so close, looking at her so intently. She swallowed. "The church's Christmas craft fair is tomorrow after the service. We could go to that together."

"And how would these people know we were there together? That we weren't just friends?" His voice had gotten deeper, somehow. His eyes had gotten darker.

"I don't know, Steve," she squeaked. "Hold my hand? Put your arm around me?"

"Like this?" he asked, his voice rough as he wrapped his arm around her shoulders.

"Yes," she said, trying not to sigh, trying not to sink into him. He was her friend, and he was doing her a favor. He wasn't making a move on her with Aiden in the house. "Like that."

His gaze intensified, the space between them crackling with energy. She felt her breathing speed up.

Did he like her? Did he *like* her like her?

"Blondie," he said, leaning closer. "Chloe, I—"

Aiden picked that moment to wake up and start crying. Steve gave her a rueful smile and took his arm off her shoulders. "I've got to get him."

"Sure," she said, simultaneously disappointed and relieved that whatever had been happening between them had been cut short. She'd already been involved with one unavailable man. She wasn't going to walk right into a relationship with another.

No matter how nice, how selfless or how attractive he might be.

She was leaving for her student teaching internship in just two short weeks. She'd best not forget it.

Chapter Twelve

Steve lifted Aiden out of the crib.

What was he doing?

Chloe had come to him for help. He wasn't going to take advantage of her vulnerability.

But—man! She'd gotten so fierce and defensive of him when he'd tried to compare himself to his dad, like she really cared about him, like she saw beyond all his baggage to the man he was inside.

Was it any wonder he'd felt this incredible pull toward her, like the undertow from a wave—

He shook his head to clear it. What was he thinking? Clearly, he wasn't.

He laid Aiden on the changing table and gave him a fresh diaper.

How should he handle this? Apologize? Pretend it hadn't happened? Lifting Aiden onto his shoulder, he decided he'd take his cue from her.

She was in the kitchen, putting the pizza she'd brought onto plates. "Hungry?" she asked in a voice that was bright—so bright it was almost brittle.

His heart sank. There was his cue. She didn't feel for him the way he felt about her.

There had to be something wrong with him, thinking someone as beautiful, as sweet, as talented as Chloe could possibly want to be with someone like him. Someone whose business was failing, whose father was in prison, who was raising someone else's son.

She'd said the things she'd said about him not being like his father because she was a nice person—not because she had deeper feelings for him.

She just wants to be friends, he told himself sternly. *Be friendly. Be her friend.*

"Looks delicious," he said, clipping Aiden into his bouncy chair before taking a plate over to the table. She sat across from him. She wouldn't meet his eye.

He needed to apologize. He needed to clear the air. "That thing," he said, "on the couch. I just—" He stopped and rubbed the back of his neck. "I didn't mean anything by it, Blondie. You're a good friend, you know?"

Was it his imagination, or did her shoulders sag, just a little?

Yep, it was definitely his imagination, because she said, "Sure, Weston. Don't worry about it. I leave for Boston in two weeks anyway, so we won't have to do this whole pretend relationship thing for very long."

He nodded. It was for the best. They wanted different things. He wanted to build a life for himself and Aiden here, on Cape Cod, and she was moving to Boston to finish her teaching degree…and maybe even find a man she could marry someday.

Just thinking about her going on a date with somebody else—let alone marrying some other guy—made him feel restless and itchy. He'd given up on the idea of getting married a long time ago, but what if he could find someone who'd accept him in spite of what his father had done?

What if he'd already found her? What if Chloe was "the one"?

But she was leaving. She was finally going to fulfill her dream of becoming a teacher, and he wasn't going to be an obstacle standing in her way.

When Chloe smiled, though… When she laughed… When she looked at him with those wide, dark eyes, it was like his heart lit up from the inside out, and he wanted nothing more than to find out what life would be like with her by his side.

He wasn't an idiot, though—he knew that, if he pursued her, it wouldn't end well. One way or another, he'd end up getting hurt.

"So, the craft fair," he said, picking up his slice of pizza. "Tell me about that."

"Oh, it's fun," she replied, her countenance brightening. "There's a bake sale and crafts, and they do tons of games for the kids. A snowball race with marshmallows, a feed-the-reindeer beanbag toss, a Frosty the Snowman game where the kids wrap each other up in toilet paper. It's always a good time."

He took a big bite of pizza. She'd gotten them a specialty pizza with olives and artichokes, spinach and sun-dried tomatoes, and pine nuts and feta cheese. It was outstanding. "Nice."

"The whole town goes, so hopefully Dan and Marissa will make an appearance, too."

"Are we going to tell *everyone* we're together, or are we just putting on a show for the two of them?"

She fidgeted in her chair. "I think it'll be better if everybody thinks we're together. That way we're not risking anybody inadvertently saying something to the contrary at the potluck."

"So, Irene and my aunt, too?"

"Yeah, everybody."

"Even Brett?" he pressed.

She shifted in her seat again. "If you don't want to do this…"

He touched her hand to reassure her, but all it did was fire his feelings for her back up. "I want to do this, Blondie. I want to help you. I just want to make sure we're on the same page. Your brother already has reservations about me, and Irene's pretty sharp…"

She snorted. "Let me worry about Brett. And trust me, Irene will be thrilled. She told me last Sunday, and I quote, 'babies need a mother.'"

Aiden punctuated the sentiment by kicking in his bouncy chair, making the toy bar rattle.

"Oh, you agree with that, do you?" Chloe asked in her high-pitched, baby voice, leaning down to unclip Aiden from his chair and then settling him in her lap. "I wish you had a mommy, too, big boy. But at least you've got a great dad."

Steve almost choked on a sip of water, he was so surprised she saw him like that. He was doing the best he could, but he was certainly no parenting expert. She'd seen that firsthand.

He honestly wasn't sure he could take much more of this conversation. It was like his heart was on some roller-coaster ride, rising to peaks of joy and then plunging straight to despair.

You're in love with her.

The thought hit him like a lightning bolt.

Without even knowing it, he'd probably been half in love with her for the last eleven years, and the more time he spent with her, the more he liked—no, *loved*—the woman she was now. Kind. Generous. Sweet, but also a little fiery. Willing to go above and beyond for anyone who needed her, but also unafraid to speak her mind.

Man, you are in so much trouble. She's leaving, and she just wants to be friends.

He stood abruptly, his chair nearly toppling backward onto the kitchen floor. "Well, um, we've got a busy day tomorrow. I'm sure you've got things to do."

"Oh, right. Let me just clean this up." She put Aiden back in his bouncy chair, then got up and cleared her plate.

She started to run the water into the sink to wash it, but Steve stopped her. "Leave it, Blondie. I'll take care of the dishes later."

She turned off the water and leaned on the counter. "Can I ask you something?"

"Sure."

"At the hospital, Mabel mentioned something about a parole hearing…"

Steve pinched the bridge of his nose. "Did she," he said. It wasn't a question. His voice was flat.

"How is that possible? Don't people go to prison a lot longer than that for—"

"The prosecutor decided it wasn't premeditated. They pressed lesser charges."

"Oh." She nodded. "Right." But she made no move to leave. "Do you have to go? To the hearing?"

Steve shook his head. "Only if I want to read a statement."

She brushed her bangs out of her eyes. Her fingers were long and delicate. He caught himself admiring them and snapped his gaze away. Friends didn't wax poetic about other friends' hands.

"What kind of statement?" she asked.

"One about how what he did has affected my life."

She nodded again. "Are you going to?"

He thought about last weekend's church sermon, and the letters his father had written to Eloise. *But if ye forgive not men their trespasses, neither will your Father forgive your trespasses.* "I don't know."

"When's the hearing?"

"End of February."

"I can probably take a day off from the student teaching job if you want me to go with you. You know, as moral support."

"Um…"

"If not, that's okay, too. I just want you to know that I really appreciate what you're doing for me with this whole Dan situation. If there's ever anything I can do to return the favor, just let me know."

"Okay," he said, but he didn't want her to feel like she owed him a favor. That wasn't why he'd agreed to help her out. "Will do."

She finally moved into the entryway and put on her shoes. "See you tomorrow, Weston."

Steve raised his hand in a farewell wave, then stood in the doorway for a long time, watching as her taillights moved farther and farther away.

Chloe met Steve and Aiden at church the next morning. She wanted to practice acting like a couple before the craft fair got underway, but Steve was jumpy. She leaned into him, and he leaned away. She brushed her fingers against his, and he practically leaped out of the pew.

"Everything okay?" she whispered, wondering if she should be offended. He hadn't seemed so loath to get close to her yesterday when they'd been sitting on the couch. But maybe she'd misread that whole situation. Maybe he hadn't been about to kiss her, after all.

Or maybe he likes you and he's not thrilled that you're just using him to placate Dan's wife.

She brushed that thought aside. He knew she was leaving for Boston soon. He'd agreed to help her because he was her friend, nothing more.

"Fine," he whispered back, stroking Aiden's hair. "I just feel weird about playacting when we're in church."

"Are you sure you really want to do this?" she asked.

"Are *you* sure?"

She nodded. "I think so."

"Then we're doing this," he whispered decisively. "And you *don't* owe me any favors."

A few minutes later, the church service ended and Steve took her hand to lead her outside to the front lawn, where there was a huge tent set up for the craft stalls and bake sale, and a smaller heated tent with a bouncy house for the kids.

"I really appreciate this, Weston."

"Do you think they'll be here?" he asked, scanning the area as though he could spot Dan and Marissa, although he had no idea what either of them looked like.

She shrugged. "If not, we can leave early. Stop in at the hospital and bring Mabel some pie."

Up ahead, Brett and Jonathan were standing by the entrance to the bouncy house, helping the little kids crawl in and out and making sure there weren't too many people inside at one time. "Sis," Brett said slowly, looking pointedly at where her hand rested in Steve's.

"Bartholomew," she said sweetly, not stopping to chat. He'd give her grief about Steve, and Chloe didn't want to hear it. Not until Dan and Marissa were gone and she could admit it was just pretend.

It was busy inside the main tent. There were stalls selling hot apple cider, hot chocolate and popcorn. Stalls selling cookies and cakes and apple pies. There were Christmas crafts, children's crafts and religious crafts, as well as beautiful themed Christmas trees that had been put up for silent auction, and wreaths galore.

In one corner, there were kids making ornaments out of Popsicle sticks. In another, kids were dancing underneath a bubble machine set up in front of a fan. In yet another corner, there was a cookie decorating station where kids were going to town on Santa-shaped sugar cookies, loading them up with icing, sprinkles, candies and dried fruit.

They did a quick walk-around, but then it was time for Aiden's next bottle, so they found a spot at one of the tables set up in the middle of the tent and fixed him one.

Once Aiden was settled in Steve's arms with the bottle, Chloe asked, "How'd he sleep last night?"

"Decent," he said. "He got up three times, but

he went back to sleep pretty quickly after I fed him. So not too bad."

Three night feedings sounded like a lot to Chloe, and she felt bad that Steve was getting so little sleep. "Have you tried a pacifier yet?"

"I've tried. He doesn't get it, though. Won't keep it in his mouth."

"Have you tried *holding* it in his mouth?"

He gave a little chuckle. "Yup. Just makes him try harder to spit it out."

"I was reading that reverse psychology can sometimes work."

He quirked an eyebrow. "Reverse psychology for babies? How does that work?"

"Instead of pushing it in, wait until he sucks on it, then try to pull it out."

He laughed. "What?"

"Just gently. Don't actually pull it out. But if he thinks you're trying to take it away, it might make him suck harder."

"Where were you reading about this?"

"A baby blog." She'd been doing a lot of baby research lately. She knew Steve worked hard during the day, and she wanted to help him out. "Worth a try, right?"

He smiled. "You're always looking out for us, Blondie. You're the best."

The way her heart leaped at his words made

her uncomfortable, so she laughed and did a curtsey to deflect. "I try."

Emma came running over, with Laura hot on her heels. The little girl had icing *all* over her face. "Mr. Steve, can I see the baby?"

Aiden was down to the dregs of his bottle, so Steve lifted him onto his shoulder for a burp and then flipped him around so Emma could see his face. "Babies this small don't know how to smile yet, but look how he's watching you. That means he likes you," he said.

"Ohhhhhhh," Emma breathed. "I love him! I love him so much!"

"Maybe you'll have your own little brother or sister one day," Chloe said, nudging Laura, who blushed.

"Can I, Mommy? Can I, pweeeeeeease?"

"We'll see, honey," Laura said.

Brett and Jonathan walked over and joined them. Brett cleared his throat. "Chloe, can I talk to you for a second?"

She leaned forward, elbows on the table. "Sure."

"Alone," Brett said, flicking a glance at Steve.

Chloe frowned. "All right."

She followed her brother over to the silent auction tables. He turned to her, arms crossed. The expression on his face was at odds with the Christmas tree he was standing next to, which was decorated with dozens of Santa's helpers sporting sunny smiles. "What are you doing?" he asked.

"What do you mean, what am I doing?" she said, acting deliberately obtuse. "I'm hanging out at the Christmas craft fair, same as you."

"The man has a baby, Chloe."

She felt her own expression darken. "I know he has a baby, Brett. I take care of Aiden every day."

"You can't mess around with a single parent's emotions. It's not fair."

Her face went hot. "*Me?* You think *I'm* messing around with *Steve's* emotions?"

Brett stared down at her, solid and uncompromising. "Well, what else am I supposed to think? You're leaving for Boston in two weeks. If this is payback for him leaving you all torn up in high school, gotta tell you, it's not okay."

"Payback? Wow. You're in rare form today." She tossed her hair over her shoulder, channeling a confidence she didn't feel. "Maybe we're both just enjoying each other's company."

"What're you going to do when you leave for Boston? You plan to keep seeing him?"

"Not that it's any of your business, but no, probably not. It's not that serious."

Brett clicked his tongue. "Does Weston know that?"

Chloe put her hands on her hips. "Yes, Brett. He is fully aware that I'm leaving in two weeks, and that I probably won't come back."

"I don't know, Chlo. The way he looks at you…"

Not this again—her brother was as bad as Laura. He was simultaneously irritating the stuffing out of her and putting all kinds of weird ideas into her head. "It's fake, Brett. It's all fake."

His eyebrows snapped together. "What do you mean, it's fake?"

"I ran into Dan and his wife at The Baby Boutique. They're staying at The Sea Glass Inn for Christmas. I asked Steve to be my fake boyfriend so I could save face in front of them. He's just doing me a favor."

Her brother made a sound that was suspiciously close to a growl. "I seriously don't know how that guy thinks it's a good idea to show his face around here after what he did to you."

She grabbed his arm. "Don't go all Neanderthal on me, okay? Steve and I have it handled."

"Did Laura know about this?"

Chloe shook her head. "I called and asked her, but they hadn't checked in yet, and she had no idea. Apparently, Dan's wife made the reservation. And besides, do you know how many Dan Smiths there are in the world?"

"Unbelievable." He smacked his fist into his palm. "Want me to go have a word with the guy?"

"Don't. Please. Just leave it alone. Steve and I can deal with it. I promise."

Brett scowled. "Are the newlyweds going to be at the potluck?"

"Probably."

"Can't Laura tell them they're not welcome?"

"And risk her livelihood and the inn's reputation? I wouldn't ask her to do that."

Her brother sniffed. "I would."

"I told you I have it handled, okay? As long as you don't tell anyone that Steve and I aren't the real deal, everything will be fine."

He smoothed a hand over his jaw and tipped his head from side to side, considering. "I don't like it, sis."

"I don't like it, either, but it is what it is. I'm not going to let them spoil things by driving me away from my own community on Christmas Eve."

Her brother stared at her for a long moment, then sighed. "Be careful, Chlo. Weston's not a great actor. Remember how terrible he always was in those church camp skits?"

Chloe laughed. She'd forgotten. He *had* been pretty bad. "We're just friends, Brett."

"You're just his friend, but him? It's obvious he's hoping for more."

"He's not."

Her brother gave her a wry look. "And you know this because…?"

"He told me. Yesterday afternoon. And, anyway, he's not interested in getting married, so there's nowhere for it to go even if he did want more. But he knows I'm leaving. He knows we're just friends. So, could you please drop it now? Neither one of us is going to get hurt."

Brett held up his hands. "If you say so."

"Thanks." She slid her arm through his elbow. "Now come on, I know you want some of Irene's coconut-peppermint pie."

Chapter Thirteen

After Chloe walked off with Brett, Aiden squawked a few times, and Steve did a quick diaper check. He took Aiden out of the tent and into the church proper to change him.

When they came back, Chloe was waiting for them at the table, two pieces of pie in front of her.

"Want some?" she asked, pushing a plate across the table toward him.

"What is it?" he asked suspiciously. It looked like a pink, goopy mess.

"This one's cranberry eggnog," she said, pointing to the slice in front of her, "and yours is candy cane pie. Oreo cookie crust and peppermint marshmallow filling."

He pushed it away. "No, thanks."

"Irene made both of them. I can vouch for their deliciousness. And Bill Anderson is over there in the booth with her, helping to make the sales." She tipped her head in the direction of Irene's pie booth, a vaguely self-satisfied look on her face.

Steve glanced over. He recognized Bill from the hospital. "And this is noteworthy because…?"

"He's had a crush on her for ages, but she won't give him the time of day."

Poor Bill. Steve could relate. "Why not?"

Chloe shrugged. "She keeps saying she's too old for him, but that's a total cop-out. In her mind, she's still twenty-five." She took a bite of the top layer of her pie, closing her eyes to savor the silky eggnog whip. "Personally, I think she's scared. Losing her husband was hard on her. I don't think she wants to go through that again."

"Can you blame her?" Steve asked, eyeing Chloe's pie. It looked much more interesting than his, especially given the rapturous look on her face when she'd taken a bite.

"No, I get it. It's a shame, though, because he's a great guy."

Steve reached over and snagged a bite of her dessert.

"Hey!" she protested.

He pushed the candy cane pie toward her and smiled. "You can have some of mine."

She shook her head. "I'm stuffed, actually. You don't want to know how many pies I sampled. Maybe we can go for a walk? Work off some of the calories?"

"Don't you want to hang around and see if we spot your ex and his wife?"

She waved her hand. "I don't think they're here. And even if they are, so what? We'll still have to go to the potluck together. It's not like seeing them here will save us from that."

Funny, she wanted to be saved from going to the potluck with him, while it felt like the highlight of his year. *More evidence that she doesn't see you as anything more than a friend.* "Sure." He got to his feet. "We can go for a walk." They exited the tent. "Where to?"

She pointed down the road. "Cemetery?"

"Kinda creepy, Blondie," he said, hoping to make her laugh.

She gave his arm a playful push. "It's peaceful."

He spread his hands. "If you say so."

They walked to the graveyard, which was next to a par three golf course. The ground was sandy, the old, thin tombstones covered in green-and-orange moss. It was quiet, save for the sound of squirrels running through the trees and the occasional satisfying thwack of a golf club connecting with a golf ball.

Aiden had fallen asleep in the wrap on Steve's

chest, his pink lips parted to show his moist, pearly gums.

Chloe slowed down to study one of the graves. "Do you think we'll get snow before Christmas?"

Steve looked up. It was overcast today, but the temperature wasn't cold. "I doubt it."

Chloe sighed and brushed her hand over the top of one of the gravestones. "When I was little, my dad used to take me and Brett here for walks on the weekend so we could practice our math."

His brow creased. "Math in the cemetery? How did that work?"

"We'd walk down the aisles and he'd quiz us about how old each person was when they died."

He chuckled. "Creative."

"He'd make it a competition, too. Whoever was fastest with the right answer got the point, and whoever got the most points won a prize."

"Didn't Brett have the advantage, since he was a year older than you?"

She smiled. "You'd be surprised how much beating your older brother can motivate a girl."

"What was the prize?"

"A quarter."

He snorted. "So, it was really just about the bragging rights."

"Hey, I spent each and every one of those quarters. I'd even split the money with Brett."

"What could you buy with a quarter?"

"Um, did you not notice the penny candy bins at The Candy Shack?"

He laughed. "Aha. I finally understand why you moved in with Irene."

She shook her head in mock dismay. "I will never understand how you had the run of the place and you didn't even try any fudge!"

"No way will you ever get me to eat roast beef fudge," he replied, laughing again. "Any other weird family traditions you want to share?"

She put her hands on her hips. "My family was *not* weird."

"You know you were totally weird. All the best families are."

Her face softened. "My dad used to pay us a quarter for every minnow we caught in a bucket, so we spent a lot of time trying to do that when we'd go to the beach."

"Your dad had you well trained. Did you ever catch any?"

She laughed. "I think it was just his sneaky way of keeping us occupied when we got tired of swimming, collecting seashells or digging holes."

"Sounds like your dad was a smart guy."

She got a wistful look in her eyes. "He was. He really was."

Steve didn't want her getting sad. "I was a math geek, too, ya know."

"You were not."

"I was," he insisted, chuckling a little. "Math geek, chess geek." He pointed his thumbs at himself. "Big-time nerd."

"You weren't nerdy the summer you were here."

He grinned. "Had you fooled, did I?"

"Guess so," she replied easily. "So, what happened to snap you out of nerdom?"

"Who says I'm not still a nerd?"

She gave him a skeptical glance. "Oh, come on. Look at you. You know you're not a nerd."

His whole body went still. Did that mean she thought he was attractive?

Maybe she hadn't completely friend-zoned him. Maybe he still stood a chance.

He smiled and put his hand over the baby wrap on his chest. "Aw, Blondie. That might be the nicest thing anyone's ever said to me."

"Don't let it go to your head, Weston." She poked him in the arm. "You know what I mean."

He held up his hands. "All right, all right. But you're not a nerd, either, despite your math-in-the-cemetery ways."

"Why, thank you, kind sir," she said, curtseying like some fairy princess, and he was struck again by how much he enjoyed spending time with her. It didn't matter what they were doing—walking in a cemetery, doing exercises for her back, changing Aiden's diaper—whenever she was around, he felt happy.

"Any other weird traditions?" he asked.

"Well, we did the whole matching Christmas pajama thing."

"That's not weird. I'd be worried if you *didn't* do matching Christmas pajamas. What else?"

"Um, I don't know. My mom would put green food dye in the toilets on St. Patrick's Day to make it festive."

He laughed. "See? That's what I'm talking about."

"At Christmas, I'd mash up all my food into a big pile and eat it all mixed together. Brett and I were going to invent 'Christmas-in-a-Can,' where we'd puree all the holiday food and put it in a spray can, like spray cheese. We thought we'd make a fortune."

He made a face. "Wow, yeah, that's probably a thousand times grosser than roast beef fudge." But her strange and quirky tastes somehow made her more endearing. She was one of a kind, like the most intricate snowflake. Unique.

"I still kind of like it all mixed together. Mashed potatoes, turkey, gravy, stuffing, cranberry sauce."

He mock shuddered. "So, I should ask Laura *not* to seat me next to you at the potluck, is that it?"

She grinned and gave his arm another little

push. "You can't ask for all my weird memories and then shame me for them!"

"I'm not shaming you."

"Then what are you doing?"

He tapped her forehead. "Just trying to understand what makes you tick."

Her breath hitched at his touch, and his heart did a funny somersault in his chest. Did she feel it, too, this connection between them? Or was it all in his head?

And how could he steer the conversation such that he could find out?

"So, your parents…" he asked. "How'd they meet?"

She gave him a self-conscious smile. "High school sweethearts."

"That's cute," he said. "How long were they married?"

"Twenty-five years. I used to catch them dancing in the kitchen sometimes. Totally weirded me out."

He chuckled. "Really? Sounds pretty nice to me. To be with someone for that long and still want to dance with them."

She gave him an odd look. "Thought you weren't looking for anything long-term, Weston."

"Things change," he said, hoping she'd take the bait. When she didn't respond to that, he asked, "Are your parents buried here?"

She brushed her hair out of her eyes and gave a small nod.

"Ah," he said. "Show me?"

She took him to their gravesite. There was a rainbow-colored pinwheel in the flower holder. He wondered if she'd brought it for them. He wondered how often she visited their grave.

Her parents had a shared tombstone, engraved with their names and birthdays and the shared date of death. The inscription on their grave read *Devoted in life, undivided in death*.

He swallowed. He wondered how that would work for his parents. If his father had truly repented, as his letters to Eloise had indicated, would God really allow them to be together again?

Would his mother want that? Would she have forgiven him? Would she want Steve to forgive him, too?

Beside him in the cemetery, Chloe was getting emotional. "You okay?" he asked, his voice pitched low.

She used the backs of her knuckles to surreptitiously wipe the tears from the corners of her eyes. "I miss them," she whispered.

He put his arm around her, drawing her to his side, and heard her give a shuddering breath. "I know."

They stood like that for a while, her face

pressed into his shoulder, his heartbeat slow and steady as he offered her his strength.

When her breathing evened out, he said, "I remember the day your parents came to that skit you were in. They were so proud of you."

The sky had clouded over, but as she looked up at him, her beautiful brown eyes still flashed in the light. "You remember that?"

"I remember a lot of things from that summer," he said quietly, holding her gaze.

She looked at him, then turned away. Was she remembering that last night at church camp, too? When the bonfire was burning low and the other kids had wandered down to the water? When he'd run his fingertips across her cheek as he'd told her she was the most beautiful girl he'd ever seen?

He was just about to tell her that he'd only said what he'd said about not wanting to get married because she was the only woman he'd ever loved—the only woman he ever wanted to marry—and he thought he'd lost her eleven years ago when his father had ruined everything else in his life. But before he could open his mouth to tell her, she gasped as a huge, round raindrop fell right on her face, followed quickly by another and another.

"Tell me you have an umbrella in the diaper bag!" Chloe squealed, holding her hands over her head in one of the most adorably ineffective gestures ever.

"Unfortunately not," he replied, zipping his jacket all the way up over Aiden's head, grabbing her hand and running back to the church parking lot.

Wet and shivering, she jumped straight into her car and took off before he could say another word.

He was soaked, too, but his jacket had kept Aiden dry, so he clipped the boy into his car seat and headed home, hoping he'd have another chance to talk to Chloe about his feelings for her before too long.

On Monday afternoon, Chloe took Aiden to the hospital to visit with Mabel. Steve arrived a little after five. She was about to hand him the baby and go home when Mabel's doctor came into the room and announced that he was going to discharge her the next morning. "We want you up and back to your normal routine as soon as possible," the surgeon explained, "not lying around in a hospital bed."

"Is it safe for her to go straight home, though?" Steve asked, his brow creasing. "She lives alone."

The doctor set down his tablet so he could give Steve his full attention. "The best way to promote an effective recovery is to give people their independence."

"But what if she falls again?"

"Steven," Mabel protested from her inclined bed, "I'm sitting right here."

"I know you are, Aunt Mabel," he replied, turning to her. "You don't want to go home yet, do you?"

"Well, I don't want to stay here."

"I can look into local rehab hospitals," Steve said, "or I can call some assisted living facilities—"

"No." Mabel's voice was clear and final.

Steve looked confused. "No to assisted living, or no to rehab?"

"I don't want strangers fussing over me, Steven."

"What about an in-home health care aide?" the doctor chimed in. "You'd have control over who you hired, and you'd get to stay at home."

Steve's brow furrowed. "Aunt Mabel, I don't know about your finances, but—"

Mabel's eyes glittered. "What if I moved in with you, Steven?"

Steve went still. "Um, what?"

"You have that third bedroom. There's plenty of room. I'll even pay you rent."

"But I work all day. And Aiden's up half the night."

"Chloe's home during the day. And I sleep with earplugs. I won't hear him after I go to bed."

The doctor leaned back against the counter in the corner of Mabel's room. "Might be a good short-term solution. Patients who live with others are generally happier at the two-week mark than patients who live alone, although by three months there's no appreciable difference between the two groups."

Steve looked back and forth between the doctor and his aunt, obviously unhappy. "Chloe's only here until the new year, and she signed up to be Aiden's nanny, not a home health care aide."

"From what Dr. Chen said, it sounds like I'll probably be able to go home without any trouble by the new year. And you don't mind keeping me company, do you, Chloe? I won't be a bother."

Chloe's eyes widened in astonishment as she realized they wanted her to weigh in on this. "Oh, um…"

"You can't just spring it on her like that," Steve admonished.

Mabel gave him a placid look. "Then you two go talk it over."

Steve touched Chloe's elbow. "How about I walk you to your car?" Then he glared at Mabel. "You're not getting an answer tonight."

They walked into the hallway. Chloe had Aiden secured in the baby wrap. Steve gestured at him. "Want me to take him?"

"No, I've got him." A couple of nurses walked by, their shoes squeaking on the freshly cleaned hospital floor.

Steve guided her toward the elevators then ran a hand over his hair. "I'm sorry about that."

"It's okay."

"No," he said firmly. "It's not."

"They were just trying to problem solve."

"You don't have to say yes to this."

"It's actually not a bad idea…"

Steve choked out a laugh. "It's a terrible idea."

"Why?"

The elevator dinged and the doors slid open. They went inside. "What do you mean, why? You can't be serious."

"I like Mabel, and she's offering to pay you rent to live there, which I know you could use, and—"

He narrowed his eyes. "Did you say something to her? About my financial situation?"

She shook her head. "Of course not. You asked me not to say anything, and I haven't."

He studied her for a long moment, as though trying to decipher whether or not she was telling the truth. "I'm not going to make my aunt pay rent to live with me."

"Why not?" she demanded. "It's a win-win. You get help paying off the money you owe, and she gets help while she's recovering."

"I'm just… That's not—" He stopped and rubbed the back of his neck. "That's not what families *do*."

"What?" she challenged. "Help each other?"

"Blondie…" The elevator started its descent.

"If I can help, I'm happy to do it. Besides, I owe you one."

"You don't owe me anything. I don't want your ex or his wife bothering you."

"And I don't want your aunt going back to her house all alone when I'm perfectly capable of stepping in to assist."

"You're leaving in less than two weeks," he said, holding up two fingers.

"Better than her being alone for that time, isn't it?"

He tipped his head back and stared at the elevator's ceiling. "Sometimes you're too nice for your own good."

She wasn't quite sure how to interpret that. His tone made it sound like an insult, but being nice was a good thing, wasn't it? She was just trying to help him out.

But maybe he really didn't want his great-aunt moving in with him. Maybe he was afraid she'd cramp his style.

Why he'd be worried about that if he wasn't dating, Chloe wasn't sure, but there had to be some reason he seemed so vehemently opposed to an arrangement that could solve—or at least mitigate—his money woes.

"If you don't want her moving in with you, that's fine. Just please don't use me as your excuse."

He stared at her, his blue eyes so dark they almost looked black.

"What?" she said, getting uncomfortable when he didn't look away.

"I would *never* use someone else as an excuse to get out of something I didn't want to do."

"Oh."

The elevator reached the ground floor and they stepped out. Steve took her arm and steered her over to the Christmas trees near the entrance. He was much taller and stronger than her, all height and breadth and muscle, but though his grip was firm, it wasn't tight, and she knew he'd never hurt her.

Her heart was racing, and for a quick second, she wondered what he'd be like with a woman he was really dating. Would he be possessive? Protective? What would it feel like, she wondered, to belong to a man like him?

Whoa. Where had *that* come from? She quickly pushed the thought aside.

"Is that the kind of guy you think I am? Someone who tries to weasel his way out of things?"

Had she upset him? She hadn't meant to. She didn't want him to be angry with her. "Of course not." She shook her head, her bangs falling in her eyes.

"Look, I know I left you hanging when we were teenagers, and I regret how I handled that. But I'm not someone who shirks his responsibilities or tries to get off easy. That's my father, Blondie, not me."

Aiden squirmed against her chest, and she put her hands on his back through the wrap in an attempt to soothe him. "Steve, I didn't—"

"You're clearly a really nice person, and you obviously have a hard time saying no to people—"

"Wait. What?"

"I don't want you saying yes to my aunt just because you don't feel like you can say no."

Aiden was squawking now, and she pulled him out of the wrap, feeling stung by Steve's words. "What are you even talking about?"

"Here," he said. "Give him to me."

"Uh-uh," she said, bouncing the baby. "I've got him. Tell me what you meant by that. Why don't you think I can say no?"

"Come on, Chloe. You know it's true. Every

single thing I've ever asked of you—stay late, come early, work for delayed pay—you've done it. You do more than I ask, even, and you have right from the start. The cooking, the cleaning, buying the baby carrier, watching Aiden so I could take a nap. And that was before we were even friends."

Whatever happened to *You're always looking out for us, Blondie. You're the best*? She'd liked yesterday's reaction to her help much better. "You say that like it's a bad thing. Like you wish I wouldn't."

Aiden pecked at her shoulder, clearly ready for his bottle. Steve's eyes flicked to the baby. "He's hungry. Did you bring his formula?"

"It's in the diaper bag," she said, nodding to the bag he was carrying.

"We should sit down."

She blew her bangs out of her eyes. "Maybe I don't want to keep having this conversation with you."

"Will you please at least stay until I've got his bottle ready?"

She stalked over to the chairs in the foyer and sat with a flounce, careful to hold Aiden steady.

Steve followed, then rooted around in the diaper bag until he'd located the formula, the various pieces of Aiden's bottle and the water. As he mixed the bottle, she said, "I like helping people. So sue me."

He stopped shaking the bottle and raised an eyebrow. "Thought you didn't want to have this conversation anymore."

"Don't you think it's a little hypocritical that the person who's benefitted most from my help lately is the one who's criticizing me now?"

He sighed as he fastened the top on Aiden's bottle. "I'm not *criticizing* you…"

"Oh, really? Then what exactly are you doing?"

He put the bottle on the floor and motioned for her to hand Aiden over. Once he got the baby settled in the crook of his arm, he plucked the bottle up off the floor and started the feeding. "I don't want anyone to take advantage of your good nature. Me or Aunt Mabel included."

Wow, it was disarming how comfortable he looked feeding the baby. As though he'd been born to hold Aiden, born to be a family man.

"So, you *do* want me to help her," she stated.

"She's *my* family, Blondie. *My* responsibility. Not yours."

"Ah, so we're back to me not worrying about your personal problems. Got it."

He sagged against the back of his chair, looking both frustrated and defeated. "That's not what I'm trying to say."

"So…what? You want to put her in a home against her wishes?"

"No, that's not what I want. Just…think about this, okay? Really think about it. Don't say yes as a knee-jerk reaction just because somebody asked or you think you owe me a favor."

"Wow, you really have a lot of faith in my decision-making process."

He sighed again. "I'm not trying to upset you. We're friends, and I care about you, Chloe. I don't want you taking on more than you can chew."

She got to her feet. It was obvious that he was being sincere, and she didn't want to continue reacting to everything he said out of irritation. "Why don't we see how it goes tomorrow, and if it's too much, I'll say so."

"If you're really sure…"

"I'm really sure," she said. "Good night."

And if she had trouble sleeping that night because she was trying to figure out exactly what he'd meant when he'd said *I care about you, Chloe*, nobody had to be the wiser.

Chapter Fourteen

Mabel was discharged from the hospital on Tuesday right after lunch, and Steve picked her up and dropped her off at his cottage before heading back to the clinic. Chloe was confident that she'd be able to help Mabel while still watching Aiden, but if she wasn't, Mabel had agreed to hire a separate caretaker. If it went well, it would be a win all around. Chloe and Mabel would have each other's company, and Steve would be able to split the cost of Chloe's time with his aunt—even if it was just for the next week and a half.

Chloe really hoped everything would go well. She wanted Steve to be able to put that money toward his clinic instead of her salary. She didn't want him to have to sell his house.

Mabel certainly hadn't been pleased to see the For Sale sign in the yard. "Level with me, dear," she said to Chloe, staring at the sign after Steve had left. "How bad is it? His debt?"

"Um…" Chloe wasn't sure how to answer. She didn't want to break Steve's confidence, but he'd clearly said *something* about it to his aunt.

"It was the funeral, wasn't it?" Mabel asked. "He wouldn't even listen to me when I said I wanted to help."

Over the baby monitor, they heard Aiden squawk, saving Chloe from having to answer. She got up and lifted him from his crib, then made him a bottle and sat at the kitchen table to feed him.

"How are the baby shower plans coming?" Mabel asked from her seat on the couch.

To be honest, Chloe hadn't made much headway since she'd run into Dan and Marissa at The Baby Boutique, although she'd come up with a few fun ideas for shower games. "How do you feel about Diaper Pong?"

Mabel was completely mystified, and Chloe had to explain that it was a game where people would use Ping-Pong paddles to hit balls into empty diapers.

"I suppose it would be fun for you young people…" Mabel conceded, although it was clear she still wasn't one hundred percent sure how the game worked.

She liked Chloe's idea of asking people to

bring diapers and formula as gifts. Hopefully, by focusing on practical presents, they could ease some of Steve's financial burden without being obvious about it.

"You don't think he'll be mad, do you?" Chloe asked.

Mabel fingered her brooch with a shaky hand. "Why would he be mad, sweetheart?"

Chloe bit her lip. "I don't know. He just seems to like doing things on his own. I'm a little worried about surprising him with the shower."

Mabel sighed. "That boy. Always thinking he has to do everything himself."

Aiden finished his bottle and Chloe lifted him to her shoulder and rubbed his back. "Was he always like that, or did it start with what happened with his dad?"

Mabel pursed her lips. "He told you about that, did he?"

"A little."

"He hates talking about that."

Chloe nodded solemnly. "I know."

"He was always so worried about his sister and how she was coping. With good reason, of course—she didn't cope well at all. But I'm not sure he ever really dealt with the fallout from it, either. He just put his nose to the grindstone and decided to be everything his father wasn't—reliable, dependable, self-sufficient."

Mabel looked down at her lap. "But you know that old saying, 'you can't heal a wound by saying it's not there'? I think that's what he's tried to do—keep slapping Band-Aids on something that needs stitches. But maybe now, with *you* here…"

Chloe smiled awkwardly, feeling uncomfortable. She wasn't going to be here much longer, and it wasn't as though Steve had brought her into his confidence because he'd *wanted* to; he'd told her because he'd been worried she'd quit as Aiden's nanny if he didn't tell her why he was running hot and cold.

And yet he'd told her last night that he cared about her, and her mind had been doing all kinds of calisthenics trying to figure out what he'd meant by that. Reading things into it. Inventing feelings on his behalf that just weren't there.

He cared about her as a friend—despite what her goofball brother had said to her at the craft fair.

And if she liked the way she'd felt when Steve had held her hand at the craft fair, if she'd taken a little too much comfort from the way he'd held her in the cemetery, if she liked the fact that he'd opened up to her a little too much… Well, those were her problems, not his.

Three days before Christmas, Steve was in the middle of a PT session with Michael Car-michael, a young guy who'd blown out the cartilage in his knee playing basketball, when his assistant interrupted him.

"Steve, your aunt's on the phone."

That was weird. His aunt never called him at work. "Hilary, can you help Mike with his quad sets?"

She nodded, and Steve went over to the phone. "Aunt Mabel?"

"Sorry to bother you at work, Steven, but it's Chloe. She was trying to get Aiden out of his crib, and she threw out her back."

He groaned. He could hear the baby crying in the background. "I'll be right there."

After confirming that Hilary could help Mike with the rest of his exercises and then close up, Steve drove home.

Inside the cottage, Mabel was sitting on the family room couch. Aiden was crying in the background. Chloe was nowhere to be seen.

"Where is she?" Steve asked.

"In the baby's room, trying to calm him down."

He went into the nursery. Chloe was on her knees next to the crib, trying to keep a pacifier in Aiden's mouth through the slats on the side. The baby, of course, was having none of it, and just kept crying and spitting it out. "I've got him," Steve said, reaching past her into the crib as she creakily got to her feet.

He'd been dying to finish the conversation they'd started at the cemetery on Sunday, but now that Aunt Mabel was here, there wasn't enough privacy to have the discussion at his house.

He needed to talk to her soon, though, because he could hardly think about anything besides her. He constantly wondered where she was, what she was doing, if she was happy, when he would see her again...

And standing this close to her wasn't helping matters, either.

"I'm sorry," Chloe said. "I don't know what happened."

"You need to rest your back. Go sit with my aunt and I'll get you an ice pack."

She hobbled out of the room as Steve bounced Aiden and tried to get him to stop crying. "Are you hungry, buddy boy? Are you wet? Do you need a nap?" He laid Aiden on the change table to check his diaper, and seeing that it was dry, picked him back up.

He walked into the family room. As he'd directed her to do, Chloe was sitting next to Aunt Mabel on the couch, looking miserable. "When was the last time he ate?" he asked.

"About three hours ago."

"Okay, so he's hungry."

"Probably."

He nodded. "On it." He clipped his screaming nephew into his bouncy chair, took an ice pack out of the freezer for Chloe and handed it to her, then came back into the kitchen to make a bottle. Fortunately, as soon as he offered Aiden the formula, the little guy started eating.

Steve exhaled into the silence then sat in an easy chair across from the couch. "So, what happened?" he asked, the baby's head warm and heavy in the crook of his arm.

Chloe gave him a sheepish look. "I lifted with my back instead of my knees."

He groaned. "Blo—" He caught and corrected himself before he could use her full nickname. It was probably too familiar, given that his great-aunt was in the room. "Chloe."

"I know," she said, still sheepish.

"Have you taken any anti-inflammatories?"

"Not yet."

"I'll get you some when he's done feeding. And if you want, we can go to the clinic and do some ultrasound therapy."

She reached behind herself to adjust the ice pack and winced. "Thanks, but I think I should just go home."

"I can take you to urgent care."

She shook her head. "This isn't my first rodeo. I know what the doctor will say. Ice, ibuprofen and stay off my feet for a few days."

"You're probably right." Aiden had fallen asleep on the bottle, a trickle of formula dribbling across his cheek. Steve carefully eased the bottle out of Aiden's mouth, set it on the side table and stood. "I'm going to put him down."

Chloe and Aunt Mabel both nodded. He left the room and slowly slid Aiden into his crib. The boy didn't stir. Then he retrieved a couple of anti-inflammatories, which he handed to Chloe once he was back in the family room.

She popped the pills into her mouth and swallowed. "Want a ride home?" he asked.

"Um…" She shot a questioning glance at Aunt Mabel.

"It's all right, dear. Aiden will sleep for at least a half an hour. Plenty of time for Steven to drop you off and come back home."

"I don't want to put you out…"

Steve shook his head. That wasn't possible. He'd do anything for her. Anything at all. "It's not safe for you to drive like this."

Chloe sighed. "I can't believe I did this again. And right before Christmas!"

He held out his hand to help her up. "Come on. We should get going."

She straightened slowly, keeping the ice pack pressed to the small of her back, and didn't fully extend her spine. "Aargh."

"Careful, dear," Aunt Mabel said.

Chloe chewed her lip, shooting Steve a piteous look. "It hurts."

"Here," he said, holding out his elbow. "Lean on me."

They walked outside and she winced as she got into the passenger seat of his car.

"You okay?" he asked, holding the door open as she settled in.

She buckled her seat belt. "Yeah, fine." He closed the door then drove slowly to her apartment so that the potholes didn't jar her back. When they got there, she frowned at the rickety back staircase.

"Do you need help getting upstairs?" he asked.

She blew her hair out of her face. "Do you mind?"

"Brace your abdominal muscles. I'm going to pick you up."

"Wait, no, I'm too—" she started. But before she could finish, he'd scooped her into his arms, *Gone with the Wind* style.

"Okay?" he asked.

"Don't drop me," she said, wrapping her arms around his neck. Her voice sounded small.

His heart rate increased. She smelled so good. Felt so soft. "Don't worry, Blondie. You're light as a feather." He started up the stairs, doing his best not to jostle her. When she sucked in a breath, he said, "Keep your core muscles braced."

"I'm all right."

At the top of the stairs, he set her gently on her feet. Evenings came early in December, and overhead, dusk was already darkening into night.

"You're so strong," she said, putting a hand on his arm to steady herself.

"Do you need help getting inside?"

She shook her head and brushed her bangs out of her eyes.

"Can I get you anything?" he asked. "Painkillers? Muscle relaxants?"

"I'll be okay," she said, rummaging through her purse for her keys.

"Don't push it tomorrow. The more you rest now, the faster you'll recover."

"I really don't want to miss Christmas," she whispered, shivering a little in the night breeze. "It was my dad's favorite holiday."

Without even thinking about it, he put his hands on her upper arms and rubbed them up and down to warm her up. "Remind me how many years they've been gone."

"Three. This time of year is hard. I get kind of down."

"Sure," he said, still standing close to her, still trying to warm her upper arms through her coat. "A lot of people do."

"Not like me, Steve. When I told you I go to

therapy? It's for this. Episodes of clinical depression. After they died, it got really bad. I basically had no interest in anything. I just wanted to stay in bed all the time and hide."

He moved his hands off her arms and carefully folded her into a hug, resting his chin on the top of her head. "I'm sorry, Blondie," he said. *I love you.*

"When I feel sad, I get scared that the depression's going to suck me under again."

"I can imagine that's very frightening."

He felt one of her hands flutter against his chest, and he lifted his head so he could see her face. "I felt that way, too, all those years ago, when you left."

Steve went completely still. His heart was pounding out of his chest with guilt and regret. "You did?"

"It was my first episode. It was awful. Nobody understood what was happening. They all wanted me to just snap out of it, but you can't really do that when there's a chemical imbalance in your brain."

He swallowed hard. "I'm sorry, Chloe. I hope you know… I never meant…"

"It wasn't your fault. It's just, for whatever reason, that was the trigger. If it hadn't been you, it would have been something else. But it scared me off dating for a long time. Having those kinds of feelings for someone, and then with the whole stupid thing with Dan…" She sighed. "Maybe I'm just not meant to be in a relationship. Maybe I'm one of those people who's meant to be alone."

"I don't believe that," he said.

And he didn't.

She was meant to be with him.

"When I said I didn't want to get married," he told her, "that's how I felt before I met you. Well, I mean, you know, met you again."

Wow, he was nervous. He hoped he wasn't ruining this with his babbling.

She looked up sharply, and the expression on her face wasn't exactly what he'd hoped it would be. "What are…? What are you saying, Steve?"

"I don't want to pretend date you—"

"But you said you'd help me with—"

"I want to date you for real."

Chloe took a step back, wincing at the pain in her back. "What?"

"I really care about you, Chloe. I've always cared about you, and I—I was hoping maybe you felt the same way."

"Steve…" She bit her lip. Why had she let him carry her up the stairs? And why hadn't she listened to Brett when he'd tried to tell her Steve was interested in more than friendship? If she had, or if she'd listened to that little voice of intuition that had been trying to catch her attention pretty much since the day she'd started caring for Aiden, she could have headed this off at the pass.

Because obviously she cared about him, too, although she wasn't sure if she cared about him as a friend or something more. Yes, she was attracted to him, but if Brett was right and God had put the desire to teach in her heart, then she *couldn't* care about Steve as more than a friend. If she did, she wouldn't want to leave Wychmere Bay. And she *had* to leave Wychmere Bay. If she didn't get her teaching degree now, she never would, and she was tired of letting her dreams slip through her fingers.

She had to fight for what she wanted. No one else would do it for her. She couldn't let someone else's wants and needs come before hers yet again.

"You don't have to answer right now," Steve said, a pained smile on his lips, and she realized she must have been quiet for an awkwardly long time. "If you need some time to think about it, that's okay."

"We're *friends*, Steve."

He ran a hand through his hair then looked at her, his eyes full of emotion. "What I feel for you, Blondie—it's not how I feel about my friends."

A thrill shot through her at his words, at the look in his eyes, at his gruff tone of voice, but this wasn't what she wanted right now. The timing was all wrong.

She knew herself: if she got involved with him now, she'd put him and Aiden first, and she'd put off earning her teaching degree *again*.

"But I'm leaving town, Weston."

"I know." Then, in a quieter, rougher voice, he added, "But Boston's only two hours away."

How could she explain this? "It's not just the distance. It's— Student teaching is really involved, and I'm going to be so busy, and I have no idea where I'll get a full-time job after I graduate. And you have Aiden, and Mabel, and your clinic…" She twisted her hands in front of her. She felt like she was kicking a puppy, and it made her feel awful. "I'm sorry, but I need to focus on getting my degree right now. Please don't be mad."

He looked out toward the ocean, a dark blanket in the night. "I'm not mad. Disappointed, but not mad."

"I'm sorry," she said again.

He shook his head. "You don't have to apologize for the way you feel."

Was it the way she felt, though? Ever since she'd started taking care of Aiden, she'd been thinking about Steve a lot, and about how she'd felt about him all those years ago at church camp.

And the other day, when she'd thought he was going to kiss her...

And tonight, when he'd carried her up the stairs...

She needed to get her head on straight. She'd been attracted to Dan, too, and look where that had gotten her. Attraction meant nothing.

Acceptance, self-sacrifice and a commitment to putting Christ at the center of a relationship—those were the things she wanted to find in a romantic partner someday. After she'd finally gotten her teaching degree.

She looked out from the landing at the stars that were starting to appear over the beach. "If you think it'll be too awkward to keep doing the pretend thing for the potluck, I'll understand."

He sighed. "Of course I'm still going to help you at the potluck, Blondie. I don't want you to have to worry about those people on Christmas."

She toed at the wood on the landing with her shoe. Why did he have to be such a nice guy? "You're making me feel bad."

He gave her a small, reassuring smile. "Don't feel bad."

"You're a great guy, Steve—"

He laughed, but it sounded flat. "You don't have to do the whole 'it's not you, it's me' speech."

"But it *isn't* you."

"You should go inside," he said. "Ice your back."

"Okay, well, thanks for helping me get home."

"Of course."

"I really am sorry," she said yet again.

He sighed. "We're good, Chloe. You're not the one who asked for things you're not allowed to have."

She cocked her head to the side. What did he mean by that? But before she could ask him about it, he started down the stairs. Over his shoulder, he said, "I hope you feel better tomorrow."

She hobbled inside to ice her back.

Chapter Fifteen

Steve closed the clinic on the twenty-third of December so he could stay home with Aiden and Aunt Mabel, and then it was Christmas Eve—the day of the Christmas pageant at church and the Christmas potluck at The Sea Glass Inn.

Mabel wanted to save her strength for the potluck, so she opted not to go to the Christmas Eve service, but Steve took Aiden. After Chloe's rejection, he needed a little hope.

He'd forgotten she'd be front and center, though, playing the piano and leading the kids in their songs. From the way she was sitting, he could tell her back was still bothering her. But, like the class act she was, she persevered.

The service started at noon and lasted about an hour. Afterward, he watched the little kids come to the altar in their costumes: Mary and

Joseph, sheep and shepherds, angels and wise men, and Emma, of course, as the Star of Bethlehem, beaming in her sparkly yellow dress with a cardboard cutout star around her face.

As Mary and Joseph made their way to center stage, holding a little doll representing Jesus, the narrator read, "'And she brought forth her firstborn son, and wrapped him in swaddling clothes, and laid him in a manger; because there was no room for them in the inn.'"

Steve glanced down at Aiden, who was awake and content in the baby wrap, peering out with his big, innocent eyes. Steve felt humbled and grateful. His mother might be dead, his sister might be gone, and the woman he loved might not love him back, but Aiden was a gift from God, just like Baby Jesus.

Steve patted the boy's back. There hadn't been any offers on Steve's cottage yet, and he still didn't know how he was going to make the loan payment on the clinic, but no matter where he ended up living or where he ended up working, he knew one thing for sure. "I'll always have room for you, buddy," he whispered to the baby. "You and me, we're family. We stick together no matter what."

The kids sang their carols, their voices young and sweet and adorably off-key. As they walked down the aisle and out of the church, the whole congregation, including Steve, sang "Joy to the World."

He waited around as the church cleared out, watching Chloe put her music away and then hug Pastor Nate. When she saw Steve, she gave him a reserved smile. It made his heart ache. He shouldn't have confessed his feelings for her. Now things would be awkward between them, which wasn't what he wanted at all.

"What did you think?" she asked once she'd reached his aisle.

"The kids did a great job. It was cute."

"How's Mabel?"

Steve adjusted the wrap on his chest. "Doing well. I'm going to swing by and pick her up on the way to the potluck."

"And you're still…" She hesitated.

"…okay being your fake boyfriend? Yup."

She let out a breath. "Thanks, Steve."

"How's your back?"

"I spent all day yesterday icing it, and I took some painkillers and a muscle relaxant this morning, so it's okay."

"Do you want to drive with us to the inn? Would that help?"

She gave him another one of those small, sad smiles. "I think I'll be okay driving. But thanks."

They walked to the parking lot and parted

ways, knowing they'd meet up again at The Sea Glass Inn in about half an hour.

Steve had never been to The Sea Glass Inn before, and it was nice. Two stories high and cedar-shingled, it sat right behind the dunes on Sand Street Beach.

Inside the inn, there was an intricate sea glass chandelier near the front door and an amazing Christmas tree in front of the sliding-glass door at the back. The dining room, where the potluck was set up, had a wood-beamed ceiling and long, farmhouse tables that were obviously conducive to large, boisterous meals.

There were lots of people there already, and lots of kids, too, running back and forth across the lawn, playing some kind of leapfrog game in the grass and eating all the appetizers. He, of course, had Aiden safely secured in the baby wrap.

After he got Aunt Mabel situated next to some of her friends in the front room, he dropped off the dinner rolls he'd brought, grabbed a can of soda and went looking for Chloe, who was all bundled up for a team game of Pictionary on the front lawn. Brett was at the drawing board, sketching a hat atop his stick figure's head.

"Santa?" someone called out.

"Fireman?"

Brett shook his head and drew another stick

figure, this one on top of a hill, then gestured at it wildly.

"King of the castle?" someone yelled.

Brett shook his head again and drew curlycues on the stick figure's feet. The timer was ticking down.

"Elf?" Chloe cried.

"Skier?" Steve called out.

Brett pumped his fist. "Yes! Steve for the win! Skier!" Then he handed off the marker and came to stand by Steve. "Good guess, bro," he said, bumping Steve's shoulder.

Steve chuckled. "You're a terrible artist."

Brett barked out a laugh. "I know, right? Good thing I can cook." He looked around then gestured toward a man and a pregnant woman walking past them to the door. "That's Chloe's ex," he whispered.

Steve studied the guy. He was tall, with dark, gelled hair, a big, expensive watch and a well-fitted blazer. He clearly had money. Was that the type of man Chloe liked? Someone slick and stylish?

"Chloe needs a good guy, Weston. Not someone who's gonna play with her heart."

Steve nodded. He hated that this guy had hurt her. He hated that she'd ever been hurt at all.

Brett clapped a hand on Steve's shoulder. "Better put on a good show today."

"Uh...what?" Steve said, adjusting one of the baby carrier's straps to buy himself a second. He and Chloe had agreed they'd tell everyone they were dating. Why would Brett think they were putting on a show?

"Listen, brother. I know you two aren't really together, but I appreciate you stepping up to help her. You're a good friend."

"Why don't you think we're together?"

Brett smirked. "Weston. I'm not blind. I know you'd date her in a hot second. She just needs a little time to catch up with you."

Did that mean he had Brett's approval? Did that mean he might still stand a chance? "You think?"

"My sister is many things," Brett opined. "Fearless is not one them."

Steve ran a hand along his jaw, feeling hopeful. "I just wish she weren't leaving."

Brett gave him a pointed look. "Is she not worth waiting for?"

"Of course she is."

"Then tell her that."

"I did." Didn't he? "But she just wants to be friends."

Brett shrugged. "I'll leave that up to the two of you. You hungry? I cooked the turkey. Want to get yourself a plate while the baby's quiet?"

Steve suddenly had an inspired idea. "Does Laura have a blender?"

Brett raised an eyebrow. "Probably. Why?"

"Chloe told me about Christmas-in-a-Can."

Brett laughed and shook his head. "Chloe and her schemes. You wouldn't believe all the weird things she's asked me to make over the years. I draw the line at Christmas-in-a-Can. Never going to happen."

Steve smiled. "You never know. Maybe it will."

He walked off to find Laura, who laughed so hard she almost fell on the floor when he told her what he wanted to do. She held Aiden while he put together a mini plate of food and blended it together in the kitchen. After he scooped the puree into a mug, Laura moved Aiden to her shoulder and said, "I'll hold on to this guy for a bit so you can go give that to Chloe. I'm glad you two found each other again. I always thought you were really sweet together."

He nodded, because what else could he do? He didn't want to break character, and he was hoping—maybe—that he could make what Laura was saying true.

He picked up the mug and went outside to find Chloe.

She was still sitting on a lawn chair watching the Pictionary game in the front yard, wearing her big pink parka, a stray marker on the table in front of her. Steve sat across from her. "Hey." He showed her the mug, holding it just out of her reach. "I brought something for you."

"What is it?" she asked, squinting at his offering. "Apple cider?"

He shook his head. She reached for the mug, and he pulled it away. "You've got to guess first."

"Cranberry punch?"

"Nope."

"Pumpkin soup?"

"No again."

"Tell me before I die from the suspense!"

He laughed.

"Come on, please tell me," she begged. "What's in the mug?"

He laughed again. "I couldn't figure out how to get it into a spray can, so *this*," he said, waggling the mug in front of her, "is Christmas-in-a-Cup."

She gasped. "You didn't!"

He grinned. "I did."

"Let me see!"

He handed her the mug. She looked inside then breathed in the scent of the pureed Christmas dinner. "Aaaaaaah. Delicious. Could you please get me a spoon?"

He pulled one out of his jacket pocket and handed it over with a flourish. "Here you go."

She took a big spoonful of the puree and licked it off the spoon as though it were ice cream. "Mmm. So good. What's in here?"

"You do realize that's worse than roast beef fudge, don't you?"

"Pretty sure I taste turkey, mashed potatoes and stuffing…"

"There's gravy and cranberry sauce, too. I spared you the veggies."

She gave him an exaggerated wink. "Good man."

He let her enjoy her weird Christmas mash for a few minutes. When she put down the mug, he said, "Brett pointed out your ex and his wife. Just let me know how you want to play it today."

She sighed. "I'm going to sit out here for a while. I don't even want to deal with them right now."

"Sure," he said. "I'll sit with you."

She looked to the sky. "I wish it would snow, but unless a big cold front comes through, I don't think it will."

He blew into his hands. "Stranger things have happened."

She smiled. "Thanks for being here, Weston. You're a good friend."

He smiled back at her, even as his heart sank

to his toes. Had he really thought his weird little offering would make a difference to her? That it would change how she saw him? That she'd know he loved her and love him in return?

Yes. Apparently, he had.

Foolishly, it appeared.

Right from the start, he'd known she was too good for him. He'd known that a romantic relationship would never work out. Still, he'd let his feelings for her overpower his common sense. He'd let his hope get the better of him, and he was paying for it now.

His phone rang and he took it out of his pocket. The display showed a New Hampshire number.

He hesitated before lifting the phone to his ear, a sense of apprehension filtering through him. The only people from New Hampshire he'd stayed in touch with were Liam's parents, and he had their number saved in his contacts list.

They weren't the ones on the other end of the line.

Chloe saw Steve pick up his phone. Then she saw the color drain from his face.

"What?" he said. "When?"

His brow furrowed in concentration as he listened to the other person speak. Then he dragged his free hand over the stubble on his jaw. "I don't think that's going to be possible. I have a kid, and I don't have anyone to watch him." He listened again. "No, I understand. I'll try. Thank you."

He hung up the phone. He stared at it.

"Who was that?" Chloe asked.

"What?" He looked at her as though he'd forgotten she was there.

"Who was that?" she repeated gently. "On the phone?"

He looked at his phone again. His expression was strange. Blank.

She stood, careful to tighten her abdominal muscles so that moving wouldn't hurt her back so much, then crouched next to him and placed her hand on his arm. "Steve? Are you okay?"

He shook his head as though to clear it. "My father had a heart attack."

She felt her eyes go wide. "In prison?"

"In prison. He's at the hospital now. They're doing an emergency bypass. They suggested I get up there right away."

"Oh, my. Do you want to go?"

He scrubbed his hand over his face again. "I can't. Your back's out. You can't watch Aiden."

"Laura will watch Aiden."

"I can't ask her to do that."

"I can," Chloe said. "Do you want me to?"

"I don't know," he said, his expression tortured. "I shouldn't want to go, should I? He killed my mother. He ruined my life."

She tightened her grip on his arm. "He's your father. If you want to go, then go."

"You really think Laura will watch Aiden?"

"I know she will."

He got to his feet, a determined gleam in his eyes. "Okay. I'll go."

"Do you want me to come with you?"

He frowned. "You can't, Chloe. Your back—"

"Will be fine," she said firmly. "I don't think you should be alone right now."

She thought he'd put up more of a fight, but he didn't. He just nodded and said, "Okay."

She found Laura, who confirmed that, of course, she'd watch Aiden, and Mabel could stay at the inn overnight, too. Then they drove to Steve's house and picked up a bunch of supplies for Mabel and the baby, as well as an overnight bag for Steve, after which they stopped by Chloe's apartment so she could quickly pack a bag for herself, too.

Laura and Jonathan met them outside when they got back to the inn.

"You'll be okay with the baby?" Chloe asked her friend.

"The travel crib's all set up, and there's plenty of formula," Laura said. "Don't worry about me."

Chloe nodded and got back in the car. Steve

turned the key in the ignition. His hand was shaking. "You've got this, Weston," Chloe said.

He blew out a breath and backed onto the road.

They drove in silence for a long time, the dark closing in, not even the radio playing. Steve seemed hypnotized by the road, and Chloe had to remind him a few times to ease off the gas. When they hit traffic on the I-93 into Boston, Steve's knuckles went white on the wheel.

"Do you want to stop for coffee?" Chloe asked.

"I just want to get there."

She closed her eyes, praying that they'd make it in time. "I know."

Another few minutes passed and she asked, "Do you mind if I turn on the radio?"

"Go ahead."

She found a radio station that was playing Christmas music and turned the volume low. After a while, she started singing along under her breath.

Once they were clear of the greater Boston area, the road opened up. "How much farther?" Chloe asked.

"About an hour."

She nodded. "Is it where you grew up?"

He shook his head. "No. We lived just outside Portsmouth. The hospital's in Concord. Near the jail."

"When was the last time you saw him?"

He clenched his jaw. "At the trial."

They reached the hospital, a blocky red-brick building. They parked the car and made their way to the information desk. The volunteer there directed them to the cardiac unit. The nurse on duty told them that Steve's father was still undergoing surgery. Steve looked at his watch in disbelief. "How long does it take? It's been hours already."

"It can take up to six hours, sir. It depends on the location of the blockages and how severe they are." She directed them to a waiting room with linoleum floors and orange vinyl chairs. "The doctor will give you an update as soon as she's able."

Chloe sat and tried to get comfortable in her chair. It wasn't easy. The chairs were hard.

Steve sat for all of five seconds and then started pacing. "I feel like a traitor."

Chloe sighed. "You're not a traitor."

"He wrote us letters. I never opened mine, but Eloise did. I found them after she died."

"What did they say?"

He sat. He ran both his hands through his hair, then rested his elbows on his knees and leaned forward. "That a couple of years into his sentence, some men from a prison minis-try came to see him. That he's been going to

AA meetings ever since. That he knows—" He stopped to take a steadying breath. "That he knows what he did was unforgivable, but that he'd like to make amends face-to-face."

He took another deep breath. "I didn't ever want to see him again, but now, knowing that he might not make it…"

"Hey," Chloe said, putting her hand on his arm and giving it a squeeze. "Don't go there. People pull through heart surgery all the time."

"I used to wish I was my buddy Liam's brother. I used to wish he wasn't my dad."

"You had a terrible childhood, Steve. I think a lot of people in your shoes would have felt the same."

He frowned and stared at the floor. "I thought God was mad at me. For a long time, I thought He was mad at me for not protecting my mother, and that He was going to make me pay."

Chloe tightened her grip on his arm. She hated that he'd felt like that. "God's not angry with you. He loves you."

"My girlfriend in college broke up with me after I told her what happened because she didn't want to be involved with 'a murderer's son.' Didn't want to marry me and risk having 'murderer kids.'"

"Well, no wonder you weren't interested in dating after that," Chloe said, trying to lighten the mood.

His expression didn't change, so she said, "Listen, I know I've said it before, but you're not your dad, Steve. You're a child of God, and your worth isn't contingent on what your earthly father did or didn't do. You're a good man and a great dad to Aiden and an awesome friend. If that old girlfriend of yours couldn't see it—"

Suddenly he was kissing her and she was kissing him back.

His hands were gentle on her face, and her arms were looped around his shoulders. Then all the reasons she couldn't kiss him rushed to her mind and she pushed him away, her hands against his chest. "No—stop. We can't."

"I love you, Chloe. I've always loved you."

Her heart seized and she had trouble drawing a breath. He *loved* her? How was that even possible? He'd only been back in her life for three short weeks.

"No," she said, shaking her head. Steve was wrong. He had to be wrong. God wouldn't do this to her again—make her choose between her dream of becoming a teacher and her dream of finding love.

Not like this. Not again. Not unless He wanted her to prove that she truly *was* the captain of her own ship, the master of her own destiny. That she wasn't a people-pleasing pushover who'd give up her calling for the first man to wander across her path. That she wouldn't say "yes" just because she didn't want to say "no." That she wasn't, in fact, too nice for her own good.

She looked Steve straight in the eye and said, "We're *friends*," before she saw the light there die.

He opened his mouth to respond but stopped when someone cleared her throat in the doorway. They both turned to look. It was a middle-aged doctor in scrubs and a lab coat.

"Mr. Weston?" the doctor asked.

Steve popped up out of his seat. Chloe followed, a little slower because of her back.

"I'm Dr. Bogle, the surgeon taking care of Mr. Howard Weston. I understand he's your father?"

"Yes," Steve said warily.

"It was a massive heart attack and a complicated procedure. He's stable now, but it's touch-and-go. You can see him if you'd like, but it's unlikely he'll wake up tonight."

Steve looked at Chloe, then at the doctor. He seemed to be at a loss.

"If you'd like, Mr. Weston, I can call the chaplain for you," Dr. Bogle said.

He looked at Chloe again. "I don't—I don't know."

"I think that's a good idea." She put her hand on his arm. She wanted him to know that she was there—that despite what had just happened between them, she was his friend and she wasn't going anywhere.

But he didn't lean into her. Instead, he stiffened at her touch. "Okay."

The doctor walked off. Chloe led Steve back to the chairs. He sat, and his expression, once again, was blank. "Are you all right?" she asked.

He turned to her, his eyes hard, and said, "I think you should go home."

Her brow furrowed, her bangs tickling her forehead. "But we came up here in the same car."

"I'm going to book a room at a motel for the night. I can get you a room, too, but I think you should call Brett and have him come get you in the morning."

"I came here to support you, Steve. I don't want to leave until you do."

He frowned. "I get it that you want to be a good friend, Chloe. But I can't do this with you right now. I can't."

"Can't do what?"

He ran a hand through his hair once, twice, three times, then looked up at her, fire in his eyes. "If you don't want to be my girlfriend, you need to stop acting like you do."

She felt her mouth drop open. "*You're* the one who kissed *me*."

"Please," he said, his voice ragged. "I just can't."

"How about we sleep on it and decide in the morning?"

He gave a short nod and they waited for the chaplain, who told Steve he'd be there all night. Then they walked to his car, found a cheap motel and booked two rooms. It was colder here than it was on the Cape, their breaths puffing out in front of them like wisps of smoke. The moon was high and hard in the sky, and the sound of the cars whizzing by on the highway was a soft, sibilant buzz, a strange contrast to the chaos jangling around inside Chloe's heart.

"You'll be all right?" she asked, feeling stricken, knowing he was heading back to the hospital alone.

"I'll be fine," he said, his voice clipped. "Good night."

She went into her motel room, sat on the bed and—without understanding why she was doing it—started to cry.

Chapter Sixteen

When Steve returned to the hospital, the chaplain offered to accompany him to the ICU. There was a police officer standing guard at the door. There was a tube down his father's throat, an IV in his hand and neck, and wires connecting him to a whole army of machines.

He looked smaller than Steve remembered. Older, too.

Steve didn't know what he was supposed to feel. Sadness? Anger? Pity? He didn't feel anything. He felt numb.

The chaplain put his hand on Steve's shoulder. "Tell him what you need to tell him, son. This might be your last chance."

But Steve didn't have anything to say. He'd come here for answers. He wanted his father to explain his actions. He wanted that terrible night to finally make sense.

When Steve didn't speak, the chaplain said, "Let's pray for him."

Steve shook his head and got up from his chair. "No," he said stonily. "Let's not."

He stalked out of the room. He felt like punching something. Why should he pray for his father when there had been no one home that night to pray for his mom?

He went into the restroom and stared at his reflection in the mirror. He wished he looked like his mother. He wished he didn't have to be reminded of the man lying in that ICU bed every time he washed his face or brushed his hair.

You're not your dad, Steve.

Maybe not, but did it matter? He still wasn't good enough for Chloe. Still wasn't good enough to be loved for who he was.

Aiden's little face flashed through his mind. The baby might not be able to verbalize it yet, but Aiden loved him. Steve was Aiden's whole family. The only person Aiden had.

Steve would love him, Steve would protect him the way the man in that ICU bed hadn't loved or protected him.

You're not your dad.

He thought about the man lying in that bed with all those tubes and wires. Who did that man have? *No one.*

He thought about the letters that man had

written to Eloise. Steve didn't know much about his father's upbringing, but he could guess it hadn't been good.

He remembered what Pastor Nate had said a couple of weekends ago at church: *We're all hurt. We're all broken. But with God's help, every single one of us can change.*

And he remembered the pageant earlier, how Baby Jesus was turned away from the inn because there wasn't any room.

Was he going to do that to his father on Christmas? Leave him outside in the cold to recover—or not—all alone?

Make room for forgiveness, something deep inside him whispered. *Make. Room.*

Steve studied himself in the mirror again. He could make enough space in his heart to pray for his father, couldn't he? One time. One prayer. On Christmas Eve, in case his father never woke up.

He walked back to the ICU. The chaplain was gone, but his father's nurse was at his father's bedside. She looked up when he entered. "Is your name Steve?" she asked in a hushed voice.

He nodded. She held out a beat-up envelope with his name scrawled across the front. "Normally, I don't go through my patients' belongings, but I tripped on his bag and this fell out. I knew, somehow I just *knew*, it was for you." She glanced out the door toward the police officer. "Read it fast, though. The cops might want it back."

Steve took the envelope. He swallowed. *Make room.* He opened the letter inside and read.

Dear Steve,

If, by the grace of God, you're reading this letter, I wanted to make a few things clear.

I don't blame you for not responding to the letters I wrote in the first few years after your mother died. I wouldn't have responded to me, either. If it had been me, I would have burned those letters in the trash.

For some reason, God saw fit to grace me with a new heart here in prison. There have been plenty of times I wished He hadn't, because it's been hard to look back at the things I've done through new eyes, especially when it comes to you, your mother and Eloise.

I was a terrible father, a worse husband and a bad man. I didn't mean to kill your mother that night, but I did mean to hurt her. For that, and for all the times I hurt her, and you, and your sister, I'm sorry. I know the words don't count for much, but I mean them. I am sorry.

If you're reading this, it might be the

only chance I have in this life to give you anything worthwhile. So here it is: the only thing you ever got from me was my looks. When you were a kid, I thought you were weak because you were kind and you cared about other people. The only person I cared about was myself.

Your sister told me about the man you've become in the letters she wrote. I tried to crush your spirit, but God prevailed in you. You are His son more than you were ever mine.
Your father, Howard

Steve read it three times before he looked up at the nurse, who was watching him. He swallowed past the lump in his throat. "Will you pray with me?" he asked.

The nurse nodded, and he took her hand in his left, and his father's hand in his right. *Peace, Dad*, he prayed silently. *I wish you peace.*

Chloe woke up just after seven o'clock the next morning. Her eyes were gritty and her back hurt. She wasn't sure what had roused her, because she was still exhausted. She'd cried for a long time in the night, and she still wasn't entirely sure why. The way Steve's voice had cracked after the doctor had asked if he wanted her to call the chaplain. The way his eyes had gone blank when they were waiting. The way he'd kissed her, then stiffened at her touch.

Someone knocked on her door. "Open up, sis. I know you're in there." The voice was muffled, but it had to be Brett.

She got up and opened the door. Her brother looked alarmingly awake, a Boston Bruins cap on his head, holding his shaggy hair at bay. "Merry Christmas," he said.

"What are you doing here?"

"Weston texted me last night. Said you needed a ride home, first thing."

She wrung her hands. "His dad had a heart attack. The doctor said it was touch-and-go."

"He told me."

"I should make sure he's okay," she said, trying to peek around her brother in the direction of Steve's room.

Brett put his hand on her shoulder. "Chloe," he said. "He wants to be alone."

She bit her lip. "How do you know?"

"He told me. He asked me to take you home so he could handle this himself."

She looked out into the corridor again. "But…"

Brett moved in front of her, gently guiding her back inside. "Go get dressed, Chlo. Respect the man's privacy."

Frowning, she took her bag into the bathroom to get changed. When she came out, Brett handed her a cup of coffee. "Where did you get this?" she asked.

"Picked it up in the lobby when I checked you out." He took her bag from her and carried it to his car.

"We're really going to leave without even checking on him?"

"He's a big boy. He knows what he wants."

She got into the car, still staring at the motel as though she could will Steve to come out if she just stared hard enough. "Did you talk to him?"

Her brother nodded, backing out of his parking space and pulling onto the road. It was slushy here—New Hampshire had gotten snow.

"When?"

"Last night. After he texted. Late."

"What did he say?"

Brett took his hat off and turned it around so the bill was in the back. "What I told you."

They drove for a while, but Chloe couldn't let it go. "I don't understand why he didn't want me to stay."

Brett sighed.

"What?"

Her brother took his eyes off the freeway for a second to give her a pointed look. "Remember what I said about those little cartoon hearts in his eyes way back when?"

Chloe nodded.

"They're still there."

She closed her eyes. Steve loved her. The thing she'd been trying not to acknowledge for days.

"Well, what should I do about that, Brett? Blow off my student teaching job *again*?"

He shrugged. "Not trying to tell you what to do. Just trying to answer your question."

They were quiet for a few miles and then Brett asked, "Do you feel the same way about him? Because if you're just being nice…"

Chloe rubbed her face. It had been niceness in the beginning, but now…

Was she in love with Steve?

She'd been avoiding that question ever since she'd thought he was going to kiss her when they were sitting on his couch. She was scared of the answer. Because if she loved him, didn't it mean she'd have to stay on Cape Cod and sacrifice what she wanted to help him take care of Aiden?

That's what love was, wasn't it? It wasn't just hearts and rainbows and warm fuzzy feelings. If you loved someone, you put your money where your mouth was and placed the other person's best interests ahead of your own.

And it would definitely be in Steve's best interests for her to stay and take care of Aiden.

She could even move out of Irene's place and move back in with Brett to save on rent money. If she did that, Steve would hardly have to pay her anything at all. He could put her salary toward paying down his credit card debt and, hopefully, save his clinic.

Could she do it? Give up her internship? Trade in her dream so that Steve could save his?

But what if things didn't work out? What if Steve left her again? What if she gave up her dream and he left her and she had nothing to fall back on except her brother's good graces? She didn't want to end up working at Half Shell by default ever again.

Did her hopes and dreams even matter when there was a child in the equation? Granted, Aiden wasn't her son, but if she and Steve got involved, she knew it wouldn't be long before she'd start thinking of him that way.

Maybe, four or five years from now, when Aiden was in school, she'd have time to pursue her degree once again. And maybe, just maybe, she'd be okay with that.

Because the truth was, she wasn't the captain of her own ship or the master of her own destiny. God was.

And even if she didn't understand it, God's timing was perfect. He'd known exactly what

He was doing when He'd led her—at this precise moment in time—back to Steve.

She didn't want to look back on her life with regrets, wishing she'd had the courage to follow her heart and reach for her dreams. But she had more than one dream to consider, because in addition to wanting a teaching career, she wanted a family, too.

A family that would be there for her, no matter what. The way she wanted to be there, right now, for Steve.

She glanced at her brother. She knew what she needed to do. "We have to cancel the baby shower."

"Already done. Laura's on it."

She nodded. More silence. There were hardly any cars on the road. It was Christmas morning, and everyone was home celebrating with the people they loved. "He made me a variation on Christmas-in-a-Can."

Brett snorted and shook his head. "Was it everything you dreamed it would be?"

"Not gonna lie. It was pretty good."

Brett rolled his eyes. "And you think *I'm* ridiculous."

She smiled and closed her eyes. "You are ridiculous."

She let the road noise lull her to sleep.

Chapter Seventeen

Steve didn't get back to Wychmere Bay until almost eight o'clock on Christmas night. He'd been texting Brett all day to make sure Aiden was fine and his aunt was all right. Brett had assured him multiple times that everything was under control.

When he got to The Sea Glass Inn, the Christmas lights were shining and the front windows were lit up, although the dining room windows were dark. He knocked on the door and, to his surprise, Chloe answered. She was in jeans and a thick, turtleneck sweater, her eyes glittering strangely in the light from the sea-glass chandelier overhead.

"Chloe," he said, almost as off balance as the day he'd walked into his great-aunt's kitchen and seen her holding Aiden for the first time. "What are you doing here?"

She opened the door wider. "Waiting for you."

He studied her for a second. It had been a long day and he was too tired for this, whatever it was. "Where's Aiden? Where's my aunt?"

"Laura took them to your place."

"Oh, then... I should go."

"Wait." She reached out and took hold of his sleeve. "Stay."

He looked at her hand on his sleeve. He looked at her.

"Please," she said, tugging on his arm a little.

He came inside and unzipped his jacket. The Christmas tree was lit up. There were wrapped gifts all over the floor. "Why didn't they open their presents?"

"They did," Chloe said. "These are for Aiden."

He gaped at the piles of presents. "What?"

"That baby shower I wanted to throw? It was today. Well, it was going to be today. But since you couldn't make it, people just dropped off the gifts."

"Wow," he said, amazed at the outpouring of generosity at his feet. "All this?"

"I told you," she replied. "You're part of this community now."

He looked at her again—her beautiful eyes, her gorgeous smile. He was so tired, and he wasn't going to be able to take it if she started talking about how he was such a good friend yet again.

"Do you want to go for a walk?" she asked. "There's a blood moon tonight. The tide's super low."

"I'm pretty tired." He hadn't even noticed the moon while he was driving back from New Hampshire; he'd been too wrapped up in everything that had happened earlier that day.

"Have you seen a blood moon before?"

"I don't even know what a blood moon is," he said.

"Total lunar eclipse. They're really cool. Plus," she said, pointing to the young Labrador retriever dozing on the couch, "Laura asked me to walk Emma's dog."

Well, he really couldn't refuse to do a favor for the woman who'd watched Aiden for him all night and day on Christmas. "All right. Let's go."

Chloe roused the dog and clipped her leash to her collar, then handed the leash to Steve. They walked onto the back patio, which had stairs that led straight to the beach. She started to say something, but he didn't even register what it was—he was too busy staring at the sky. "Whoa. I've never seen anything like it."

The moon was giant and mottled, hanging low and shining copper-red.

Chloe whistled. "Talk about amazing."

It was dark on the beach at night—no light pollution—and the sound of the surf hitting the sand was loud. The dog whined and pulled Steve forward, down off the patio and into the sand. He laughed and said, "Slow down, girl. Let's take our time."

They walked past the dunes, menacing in the dark, and onto the wooden boardwalk, which took them down to a rickety-looking lifeguard stand stationed in the middle of the public beach. The tips of Steve's ears and nose prickled with the cool breeze, and he noticed that Chloe was keeping her hands in the pockets of her big pink parka—presumably so they wouldn't get cold.

"Feels like that cold front blew in," he said.

She looked up and scanned the night sky. "Yes, but there aren't many clouds, so I doubt it'll snow."

"Have you seen one of these blood moons before?" he asked her.

She shook her head. "Not like this. This has to be a blood moon and a supermoon combined."

"Look at the water," he said. The tide was out a good hundred feet farther than usual. "It's like we're Moses parting the Red Sea."

The curving white-sand beach stretched roughly a mile from harbor to harbor, bordered by long, rocky jetties on each side. He'd never seen the tide out this far. The sand normally covered by the sea shimmered in the red light of the moon, wet and soft and smooth.

"Want to walk out there?" he asked. "See how far we can go?"

Chloe nodded. "I feel like we're on Mars."

"How's your back?"

"I took a painkiller and a muscle relaxant. It's okay."

They walked to where the ocean usually began, then farther, down a steep slope that gradually leveled out.

"Do you know why it turns red?" Steve asked, nodding up at the moon.

"It's an eclipse, so the moon isn't getting any direct light from the sun, but it's reflecting dispersed light from our sunrises and sunsets."

"Wow," he said. He didn't feel tired anymore. "A reflection of sunrise and sunset. That's pretty cool."

They walked out to a sandbar and climbed up it, the sand soupy under their feet, sucking at their shoes. The beach was like an alien landscape, strange and disconcerting—the glow of the red moon, the cold air, the incredibly low tide.

"So, how did everything go today?" Chloe asked, her breath turning into small white puffs in front of her face.

He didn't want to talk about it. "As well as it could go, I guess."

"Is your father…? Did he pull through?"

Steve shook his head. "He died during the night."

Her face crumpled. "I'm so sorry. I know you wanted to see him."

"It's okay. I did see him. And he wasn't alone when he passed." Self-preservation dictated that he keep the rest of it to himself, but he didn't want to. Despite all his hopes for more, Chloe actually *was* his friend, and he wanted to share this with her. "He left me a letter that explained some things. The chaplain and I talked about it this morning." He stopped and squinted at her. "Are you familiar with Galatians 5 verse 1?"

"I don't think so."

"It says 'Stand fast therefore in the liberty wherewith Christ hath made us free, and be not entangled again with the yoke of bondage.' The chaplain showed it to me. He thought it might help me let things go and move on."

She nodded thoughtfully. "I like that."

Steve did, too.

He'd actually talked to the hospital chaplain for a long time this morning about a lot of things—his dad, his business, his great-aunt, his nephew, Chloe. Interestingly, so much of what

the chaplain had said was similar to what Chloe
had been telling him these past few weeks.

You're not your dad, Steve.

You're a child of God.

There's no shame in asking for help.

Steve had wrestled with it all as he'd driven
back to Cape Cod. Could he do what Chloe,
the chaplain and even his father—in his letter—were guiding him to do? Decide that his
father's actions were his father's responsibility
and leave them be?

Decide that he was his own man, a man God
loved? A man who had nothing to prove and
nothing to hide?

He wasn't sure he'd ever be able to put the
events of his childhood completely behind him,
but he'd decided he wanted to try. His father's
sins had held him captive for far too long. It
was time to shake off that yoke and walk free.

"Will you have to pay for another funeral?"
Chloe asked.

Steve shook his head. "The department of
corrections has a fund. They'll take care of it."

"That's good."

They were silent again.

"What happened with your ex?" he asked.
"Are he and his wife still hanging around?"

"Actually, no. She started having contrac-
tions yesterday after we left. Laura said it turned

out to be false labor, but his wife was spooked enough that she wanted to go home. They're gone."

"Good."

Another beat of silence. Chloe took her hands out of her pockets. "You were pretty upset with me last night."

He sighed. Not his finest moment. "Yeah."

"I'm sorry I…" She stopped, then started again. "Did you mean what you said after you kissed me?"

He rubbed the back of his neck, stalling. He loved her, and she was leaving. He'd kissed her, and she'd pushed him away.

He should have listened to her. She'd told him again and again that she wanted to be friends— *just* friends. But his heart had clung to this wild, impossible hope that, deep down, she didn't really mean it. That, deep down, the way she accepted him, calmed him and cared for him meant that she loved him, too.

But she didn't. She'd made that clear last night when he was at his lowest. She cared about him, sure. As a friend. But she didn't love him and she probably never would. "Chloe…"

She pushed her bangs out of her face and looked up at him, her dark eyes shimmering in the starlight. "I was pretty miffed when Brett showed up at my motel room door this morning."

Steve spread his hands. "I didn't think you'd call him on your own."

"You were right." She nudged his arm with her elbow. "I wouldn't have."

"I can fight my own battles, Blondie."

"I know you can." She paused ever so slightly and that hope—that wild, vicious hope he couldn't seem to shake no matter what he did—sprang to life again. "But isn't it better when you don't have to?"

The dog whined and pulled him off the sandbar. Chloe followed him down, stumbling a little at the bottom. He reached out to steady her. Was she saying what he thought she was saying? "If this is the part where you tell me you want to be good friends, please don't."

His hands were on her waist and her hand was on his arm. "Why'd you make me Christmas-in-a-Cup, Steve?" Her voice was soft, little more than a sigh.

Please let her be saying what he thought she was saying. *Please.*

"You know why, Chloe."

"Tell me again," she said. "Please."

The hope in his heart was rising, glowing like the light of a thousand Christmas candles, swelling like the song of a blackbird at dawn. "I wanted to make you happy."

"Why?"

He'd already told her at the hospital, but he'd tell her a million times over. After all, he had nothing left to lose. "Because I love you."

She inhaled sharply, her beautiful brown eyes wide and lustrous. "Still? Even after the way I left things last night?"

"Still," he vowed, brushing her hair back from her face, which was shining like porcelain in the starlight, soft and smooth and warm. "Always."

Her eyes pooled with emotion before she broke his gaze, the tiniest hint of a smile playing on her lips. "I don't think we should be friends, Weston."

"No?" he asked, an answering smile pulling at the corners of his mouth. "What do you think we should be?" He moved his hands to her waist, drawing her closer.

She looped her arms around the back of his neck. Her face was tipped up and her eyes were gleaming. "I think I really care about you, too."

He dipped his head down and kissed her. This time, she didn't push him away.

A fierce, uncontainable joy unfurled inside him and, just like that, one of the longest, loneliest days of his life turned into one of the best.

When the dog jerked on the leash, Steve stepped away, dazed and laughing. "We've got our own personal chaperone here."

Chloe, who also looked a little off-kilter, leaned down and gave the dog's head a vigorous pat.

Steve was smiling so big, it felt like his cheeks might burst. Then he stepped closer and pulled her back into his arms.

Brushing her bangs out of her eyes, his fingers lingered on the soft skin on her face. "Have you moved into your apartment in Boston yet? Maybe Aiden and I can help you with that next weekend."

She looked away from him, toward the tiny lighthouse at the end of the jetty, its green light flashing to warn boats away from the rocks. "Brett got me thinking… If I was willing to give up the student teaching job for Dan, shouldn't I be willing to give it up for you and Aiden, too?"

Steve shook his head. "If you're asking yourself that question, I don't think you understand how I feel about you, Blondie."

She cocked her head to the side, obviously confused. "What do you mean?"

"I mean that your dreams are my dreams. Your happiness is my happiness. And I'll wait for you, no matter how long it takes."

"You'll wait for me?" she repeated, sounding stunned. "To get my degree?"

"I know I don't have much from a material standpoint to offer you, but I'll always be on your side, Chloe. I'll support you in whatever you want to do. Through thick and thin, whatever happens—always."

"Even if you have to find a new nanny for Aiden?"

He cupped her face. "I don't want you to be Aiden's nanny. I want *you*. I want your heart."

"But what about your clinic?"

He shrugged. "If it's God's will, we'll find a way. If not, I can get a job somewhere else. My job doesn't define me, just like my dad doesn't define me. It's like you said—who I really am is a child of God."

"Wow," she said, still sounding astonished. "I'm pretty wise, aren't I?"

"The wisest." He kissed her forehead. "And the kindest." He kissed her cheek. "And the most beautiful." He kissed her lips.

"Stop," she whispered. "You're going to make my ego as big as Brett's."

He laughed. "I have to get all my compliments in quickly, though, because you're going to be gone for—how long?"

"Six months," she said. "The semester starts in January and ends in June."

"Six months? That's nothing."

She arched an eyebrow. "Nothing?"

He kissed her cheek again, a feeling of lightness breaking through him, a rightness so profound he felt it down to his toes. "I've already waited eleven years for you, Blondie. I'm a patient man. I can wait a little more."

As he held her, a spot of moisture landed on the back of his neck. Was it raining? Then another and another. He looked up and laughed. "Chloe!"

She looked up, too, and gasped. "It's snowing! I can't believe it!"

"Merry Christmas, sweetheart. May all your dreams come true."

She went up on her tiptoes under the stars and the snow and the strange red light of the blood moon. "They already have." She wrapped her arms around him and pressed her face into the crook of his neck. "And for the record, I don't just care about you, Steve. I love you, too."

He squeezed her tighter. "There's no way you're getting rid of me now. You know that, right?"

She winked at him before she kissed him again. "Christmas-in-a-Cup kind of gave it away."

Epilogue

Chloe's online degree program didn't offer a graduation ceremony, so Steve and Aiden came to Boston at the end of June for the graduation ceremony for her kindergarten kids.

Aiden himself had graduated from the simple baby wrap into a legitimate baby carrier with snaps and buckles, although oftentimes he actually preferred the stroller.

He was much more alert than he'd been as a newborn—he didn't fall asleep at the drop of a hat anymore, and there was a lot more structure to his day. One-hour naps in the morning, two-hour naps in the afternoon. Five bottles evenly spread throughout the day. Lately, Steve had even started giving him a few bites of puree.

He'd been in daycare since Chloe had left in January, and every time she saw him, which was pretty much every weekend, she'd exclaim over how much he'd grown.

Today was no exception. When Steve walked into the school auditorium an hour ahead of schedule, she dropped the decorations she was taping to the walls and ran over to the two of them.

"You're early!" she cried, letting Steve sweep her up into his arms and twirl her around a couple of times.

"We missed you, love. We couldn't wait."

She knelt in front of the stroller and said hi to Aiden, who cooed and smiled at her. She unclipped him from the seat and gave him his own little twirl. "How are you, big boy? It's only been three days, but you've grown *again*!"

Aiden laughed, and Chloe set him on the floor. He could sit up by himself now, and Steve was encouraging him to crawl. "Be careful what you wish for, Weston," she'd said on her last visit home. "You're going to be chasing him around everywhere in no time flat."

"Nope," Steve had said, pulling her close. "*We're* going to be chasing him around everywhere."

"*I'm* going to be teaching kindergarten," she'd retorted, grinning. "Not chasing the babies." Aiden's daycare center was also a preschool, and Chloe had accepted a job teaching the kindergarten class starting in the fall. She'd make less money than she would have at a public school, but she didn't care. She'd be close to Steve and Aiden—not to mention Brett, Laura, Emma, Irene and Mabel—and that was what was important to her.

A lot had happened over the last six months. Mabel had sold her cottage and moved in with Steve full-time. She'd insisted on using part of the proceeds from the sale to cover the cost of Eloise's funeral. It also turned out that, since Steve hadn't co-signed for his sister's hospital stay, he hadn't been on the hook for her medical bills. Without the credit card debt and hospital charges hanging over his head, he'd been able to get his clinic back on track. Business was thriving, and they were all grateful for that.

Laura and Jonathan had married in the spring, with Chloe as the maid of honor and Brett as the best man. Irene had brought Bill Anderson to the wedding as her date, and he'd proposed to her a few weeks later, so they were now in the throes of wedding planning, as well.

In the school auditorium, Steve handed Aiden a rattle, which he proceeded to enthusiastically whack against the floor. "How can I help you?" Steve asked, turning to Chloe.

"Do you mind taping up this artwork? The parents are going to start arriving soon, so I should set out the snacks."

Steve started taping, and Chloe hurried to the

staff room to retrieve the bagels, juice and donuts they were serving at the event.

They finished setting up, the kids' parents began arriving and Chloe went back into teacher mode. She was so proud of her little students, and it was fun watching them sing songs for their parents and get their little awards, like the good friend award, the good helper, the awesome artist, and so on—one for each child.

When the ceremony was over, the kids went home and the room teacher hugged her. "You did a great job this semester, Chloe. Your new school is fortunate to have you."

The kids' parents had already taken down all the artwork, so all they needed to do was clean up the remnants of the snacks. "Don't worry about it," the room teacher told her. "Go enjoy your day."

Steve put Aiden in his stroller and pushed him outside. "Are you done packing?" he asked. "Do you need any help?"

She shook her head. "Nope. All packed and ready to go."

"I'm so proud of you, Blondie. You did it! You got your degree."

She laughed. "Well, I don't have it just yet. They still need to mail it to me."

"You know what I mean," he said, looping his arm around her waist and giving her a squeeze.

"Yeah," she said, squeezing him back. "I do."

He opened her car door and waved her inside. "Well, what are we waiting for? Let's get you home to Cape Cod."

That night, after a celebratory potluck dinner with all their friends at The Sea Glass Inn, Steve asked Laura to watch Aiden and then motioned Chloe outside. "Moon's not as big as last time," he said, "but I thought it would be nice to go for a walk."

She let him take her hand and lead her over the dunes. Near the water, a bonfire was burning, but there was no one there to attend it.

"Um," she said, looking around anxiously, "that's kind of dangerous."

"Brett set it up, sweetheart. He just left."

"Brett set it up?" she parroted, shocked that her brother would be so irresponsible.

Steve laughed. "For us, Blondie. He set it up for you and me."

She cocked her head to the side, flutters roaring to life in her stomach.

"Come on," Steve said, leading her closer, the air warm, the beach dark, the sound of the waves hitting the shore punctuating the night.

They sat beside the fire, the air above it distorted by the heat, the logs crackling. There was a blanket set out on the sand, on top of which sat a couple of roasting sticks, a bag of marshmallows and a plastic container full of what she assumed to be chocolate and graham crackers. "You did this for me?" she asked.

"I'd do anything for you, Chloe. I hope you know that by now."

"I do know it," she said, leaning into him. "I'd do anything for you, too."

He put his arm around her and stared into the fire. "The summer we met—that was the best summer of my life. And that last night—that kiss—was like a golden memory for me, this incredible moment before everything else in my life fell apart."

She tilted her face up and let him kiss her, the same as that first time, in front of the bonfire, under the stars.

"I don't want to be apart from you ever again," he said, brushing her hair back from her face and gazing into her eyes.

"I don't, either."

He'd been sitting next to her, but he shifted to kneel in front of her in the sand. Her hand flew to her mouth.

"I've felt alone a lot of my life, but I don't want to be alone anymore. Be my family, Chloe," he said, taking a ring out of his pocket and holding it out to her. "Be Aiden's mother. And please, sweetheart, say you'll be my wife."

Her hands shook as she reached for him. "You and Aiden are already family to me, Steve. Yes!"

"Yes?" he repeated as though he couldn't believe it.

"Yes, yes, yes!"

He kissed her before she could get a good look at the ring. Then he slid it onto her finger.

It was small and delicate, a ruby in the center with diamond chips on each side. "I know it's not much, but the ruby's for the bonfire where we had our first kiss, and for the blood moon on Christmas when we started dating for real."

She held her hand out in front of her and watched the ruby flash in the firelight. "I love it. It's so romantic."

He smiled and pressed his lips to hers. "I love *you*."

"I love you, too."

He picked up the roasting sticks and passed one to her. "Let's toast our marshmallows."

They held the marshmallows over the fire. He went for golden-brown, while she set hers on fire.

While she ate her blackened marshmallow, he fiddled with the container and then handed her a s'more.

"What about yours?" she asked, pausing before she lifted it to her mouth.

He smiled. "You know I don't care much for dessert."

She shrugged and took a bite. "Mmm. What's on this? Jam?"

He shook his head. He looked way too pleased with himself. "It's cranberry sauce, Blondie. Christmas-in-a-S'more."

She laughed so hard she started crying.

He kissed the side of her head. "I want to have children with you and grow old with you and watch you eat weird food forever."

She gave his hand a little pat. "You're too good to me."

"The way I feel about you—I could give you the whole world and it wouldn't be enough."

"I don't need the whole world, Weston," she said, smiling. "All I want is you."

* * * * *

Dear Reader,

Don't you love reading books about babies?

Writing this book was lots of fun, because it reminded me of when my boys (who are now seven, nine and eleven) were that little.

My firstborn had a condition called allergic enterocolitis, which made him super colicky. The poor little guy hardly napped, hated being in a stroller or his car seat, and he cried and cried and *cried*.

When he was a few weeks old, I discovered one of the baby wrap carriers that Chloe and Steve use in this book. Lo and behold, my son loved it! I'd walk around the neighborhood with him in the wrap for hours. I was grateful that I'd finally found a way to keep him calm, and to let him get some much-needed daytime sleep.

I'm grateful, too, that Chloe and Steve were able to overcome their differences and provide a new family for little Aiden. Since he's the product of my imagination, I just know he's going to grow up to be a sweet, thoughtful boy—just like my own kids!

If you'd like to see more of Steve and Chloe, I have a special bonus scene from their first meeting as teenagers to share with you. Visit meghannwhistler.com/newsletter and sign up for my email newsletter, and I'll send you the bonus scene right away. (If my email gets lost in cyberspace, which unfortunately happens sometimes, please feel free to contact me at meghann@meghannwhistler.com so I can send it to you again!)

Wishing you love, light, and
a very merry Christmas,
Meghann